SOUTHGATE

MATT AND TOM OLDFIELD

ULTIMATE
FOOTBALL HEROES

SOUTHGATE

FROM THE PLAYGROUND
TO THE PITCH

DINO

First published by Dino Books in 2022,
an imprint of Bonnier Books UK,
4th Floor, Victoria House, Bloomsbury Square, London WC1B 4DA
Owned by Bonnier Books,
Sveavägen 56, Stockholm, Sweden

🐦 @UFHbooks
🐦 @footieheroesbks
www.heroesfootball.com
www.bonnierbooks.co.uk

Text © Matt Oldfield 2022
The right of Matt Oldfield to be identified as the author of this work has been
asserted by him in accordance with the Copyright, Designs and Patents Act 1988.

Design by www.envydesign.co.uk

Paperback ISBN: 978 1 78946 574 7
E-book ISBN: 978 1 78946 575 4

British Library cataloguing-in-publication data:
A catalogue record for this book is available from the British Library.

Printed and bound in Great Britain by Clays Ltd, Elcograf S.p.A.

3 5 7 9 10 8 6 4

For all readers,
young and old(er)

ULTIMATE
FOOTBALL HEROES

Matt Oldfield is an accomplished writer and the editor-in-chief
of football review site Of Pitch & Page. Tom Oldfield is a
freelance sports writer and the author of biographies on
Cristiano Ronaldo, Arsène Wenger and Rafael Nadal.

Cover illustration by Dan Leydon.
To learn more about Dan visit danleydon.com
To purchase his artwork visit etsy.com/shop/footynews
Or just follow him on Twitter @danleydon

TABLE OF CONTENTS

ACKNOWLEDGEMENTS

First of all, I'd like to thank everyone at Bonnier
Books UK for supporting me throughout and for
running the ever-expanding UFH ship so smoothly.
Writing stories for the next generation of football fans
is both an honour and a pleasure. Thanks also to my
agent, Nick Walters, for helping to keep my dream
job going, year after year.

Next up, an extra big cheer for all the teachers,
booksellers and librarians who have championed these
books, and, of course, for the readers. The success
of this series is truly down to you.

Okay, onto friends and family. I wouldn't be writing
this series if it wasn't for my brother Tom. I owe him

so much and I'm very grateful for his belief in me as an author. I'm also very grateful to the rest of my family, especially Mel, Noah, Nico, and of course Mum and Dad. To my parents, I owe my biggest passions: football and books. They're a real inspiration for everything I do.

Pang, Will, Mills, Doug, Naomi, John, Charlie, Sam, Katy, Ben, Karen, Ana (and anyone else I forgot) – thanks for all the love and laughs, but sorry, no I won't be getting 'a real job' anytime soon!

And finally, I couldn't have done any of this without Iona's encouragement and understanding. Much love to you.

CHAPTER 1

WINNING AND LOSING TOGETHER

11 July 2021, Wembley Stadium

As the second half of extra-time ticked by, it was clear that the Euro 2020 final was only going to end in one way: with a penalty shoot-out. Everyone knew it; the exhausted players out on the pitch, the 67,000 anxious supporters in the stands, and especially the two managers on the touchline.

Yes, for England's Gareth Southgate and Italy's Roberto Mancini it was decision time. Who would take their team's first five penalties, and in what order? After hours and hours of practice at St George's Park, Gareth had worked out the answer to both of those questions, but there was just one problem: two of England's best takers were still sitting on the bench. So, with only seconds to go, he made a bold double substitution:

Marcus Rashford on for Jordan Henderson,

And Jadon Sancho on for Kyle Walker.

Right, now they were ready for penalties! Moments later, when the referee blew the final whistle, Gareth had a quick chat with his assistant, Steve Holland, and then gathered his tired players together for one last team-talk.

'You should be all so proud of what you've achieved so far,' he told them, 'but now it's time for one last push. We can do this, we can win this!'

Come onnnnnnnnnnnnnn!

After his own painful penalty experience twenty-five years earlier, as an England player at Euro 96, Gareth had worked hard to prepare his players for such a high-pressure situation. In the semi-final shoot-out against Germany, he had been brave enough to step up and take his team's sixth spot-kick, but without any practice, Gareth Southgate had struck the ball straight at the keeper.

Now, however, everything was different. Gareth had made sure that the England players knew exactly what they needed to do:

Stay calm, stay positive, stick to the plan, *SCORE!*

And what they needed to NOT do:

PANIC!

Plus, they had the confidence of knowing that they had succeeded before. At the 2018 World Cup, Gareth had led England to their first penalty shoot-out win in twenty-five years, against Colombia. They had done it once, and now they could do it again. The England manager believed in every single one of his heroes:

1) Harry Kane… placed his penalty in the bottom corner where the Italian keeper, Gianluigi Donnarumma, couldn't reach it. *GOAL!*

'Yesssssss!' Gareth roared, punching the air with passion. While the England players stood united on the halfway line, he stood with his coaches on the sidelines. It was one big team effort – they won together and they lost together.

When Jordan Pickford saved Italy's second spot-kick to give England the advantage, Gareth didn't show any emotion at all. It was too early, and he was too experienced, to get carried away just yet.

2) Harry Maguire… blasted an unstoppable shot into the top corner. *GOAL!*

Gareth punched the air again – it was all going according to plan for England so far. Their next two takers, however, were the last-minute substitutes, who had barely kicked a ball during the game. It was a risky move from the England manager – would it turn out to be a touch of genius or a massive mistake?

3) Marcus Rashford… clipped the outside of the post. *MISS!*

4) Jadon Sancho… aimed for the bottom corner, but Donnarumma dived the right way. *SAVED!*

On the sidelines, Gareth did his best to hide his disappointment, but on the inside, his heart had sunk right to the bottom of his stomach. It was all his fault; his plan had failed.

It really didn't look good for England, especially as Jorginho was next up for Italy. The midfielder almost always scored from the spot, but not this time, because Jordan dived down to make a super save.

Come onnnnnnnnnnnnn!

Phew – England were still in the Euro 2020 final shoot-out, but they had to score their fifth penalty. So, who would take it? Raheem Sterling? Jack Grealish? No – instead, Gareth had given that huge responsibility to his youngest player.

5) Bukayo Saka… aimed for the same bottom corner as Jadon, but Donnarumma dived the right way again. *SAVED!*

Noooooooooooo!

It was all over and Italy, not England, were the Euro 2020 winners. As the *Azzurri* players celebrated, Gareth went over to comfort the three devastated Young Lions, Marcus, Jadon and Bukayo. He was a manager who cared deeply about his players.

'I know it really hurts right now, but you'll come back stronger than ever,' he told them, speaking from experience. 'Remember, we win together and lose together. It was my decision for you to take that penalty and you were brave enough to step forward when I asked you to. So, be proud of yourself and don't worry, we'll be back!'

At the post-match press conference, Gareth began by taking full responsibility for the defeat: 'Penalties are my call. We worked in training. It's not down to the players. Tonight it hasn't gone for us. We know they were the best takers we had left on the pitch. Of course it's going to be heartbreaking for the boys, but they are not to blame for that.'

Gareth wasn't the kind of person, or manager, who liked to dwell on disappointments, though; instead, he preferred to focus on the positives. 'The players have given everything and I'm proud of them,' he said at the end. 'They've got to walk away from here heads held high. They've done more than any team in the last fifty years.'

Yes, although they hadn't quite managed to bring football home, Gareth's England squad had succeeded in giving the country plenty to cheer about. With their winning smiles, strong principles, and superb performances on the pitch, they had united the nation during Euro 2020, just like they had during the 2018

World Cup. It was a summer that none of them would ever forget, but this wasn't the end; no, it was only just the beginning.

Under Gareth's guidance, England were making real progress, and moving in the right direction – semi-finalists at the 2018 World Cup, finalists at Euro 2020... What next – World Cup winners?

Why not? Even at the age of fifty, Gareth was still the same boy with the big England dream.

CHAPTER 2

THE BOY WITH THE BIG ENGLAND DREAM

'Gemmill has the ball, he goes past one defender, then another, and then another! He's into the box now, with just the keeper to beat... *Goooooooaaaaaaaalllll llllll!!!!!!!!!!'*

After firing the football into the gap between two heavy flowerpots, Gareth ran over to the imaginary fans by the garden wall with his right fist raised – just like his new hero, Archie Gemmill.

'A brilliant individual goal has put Scotland in dreamland!' he shouted, copying the words of the commentator on TV.

Unfortunately, England had failed to qualify for the 1978 World Cup in Argentina, and so Gareth had felt obliged to become a Scotland supporter instead. Only this once, though; hopefully England would be back at the tournament in 1982, and then he imagined that at one future World Cup – perhaps 1990, or 1994, or 1998 – he himself would be out there wearing the Three Lions on his shirt, proudly playing for the national team. That was the big dream, anyway, as he kicked a ball around in his back garden in West Sussex at the age of eight.

Although he probably wasn't the most skilful footballer at Pound Hill Primary School, Gareth was definitely one of the most determined and energetic players in the playground. During breaktimes and lunchtimes, he raced up and down the field, chasing every ball, until the bell rang for lessons to start again.

'Gareth, go and wash your face first,' his teacher often had to tell him. 'You're drenched in sweat!'

Fitness ran in the Southgate family. Both of his parents had been athletes when they were younger; his dad, Clive, had been a talented javelin thrower, while his mum, Barbara, had been a hurdler. Gareth enjoyed athletics too – and rugby and basketball – but football was always the sport for him. Out on the pitch with his friends, he felt so happy, comfortable, alive and free. Especially when he was on the winning team!

By the time he started secondary school, Gareth was the fittest kid in Crawley. After cycling to Hazelwick every morning with his bag of books, he would then rush home at lunchtime to collect his sports kit for the afternoon, and pedal his way back as fast as he could in time for class.

Studies and sport: Gareth liked both sides of school life, but if he had to choose, football always came first. In those early years, he played for lots of different teams – his school, the cub scouts, a local Sunday league club – but whatever the colour of the kit, Gareth always imagined that it was a white England shirt he was wearing. 'The next Bryan Robson' – that's who he really wanted to be.

Four years on from the 1978 World Cup, Gareth got his wish, when England successfully qualified for the 1982 tournament in Spain. And in their first group game, they beat France 3–1, thanks to two goals from

Bryan Robson that Gareth recreated again and again during kickarounds with his friends:

'Trevor Francis crosses the ball into the box towards Robson, who jumps up high to head the ball into the net... *Goooooooaaaaaaalllllllll!!!!!!!*'

It wasn't just the glory moments that Gareth loved about Robson, though; on the football pitch, the midfielder could do it all – tackle, pass, head, shoot, and run around all game long. Robson was such an amazing all-round player that his Manchester United teammates called him 'Captain Marvel'.

'Captain Marvel' – wow, what a cool nickname! Maybe one day, people might call Gareth that too, when he was starring in the England midfield at future World Cups. He added that to his long-term plan, and in the meantime, he watched Robson in action for Manchester United on *Match of the Day* every weekend and worked hard on copying his style: the bursting runs into the box, the clever flick headers, the fist-pump goal celebrations, and most importantly, the New Balance boots he wore.

Great, Gareth was all set to be a football star, for

club and then country! But which club would he play for? Sadly, Manchester United was a long way away from West Sussex, but luckily there was another top team on the south coast of England that was much closer to home.

CHAPTER 3

STARTING OUT AT SOUTHAMPTON

Gareth was eleven years old when he first began training with Southampton. Although it was only one evening session per week, it was still a really exciting opportunity to test himself against the best young footballers in the area. Plus, it meant that he could proudly tell his friends at school that he played for a club in the First Division!

The First Division – that's what the highest level in English football was called, before the Premier League launched in 1992. When Gareth started out in the youth system in the early 1980s, Southampton weren't one of the top teams in the First Division, like Liverpool and Manchester United were, but they still consistently finished in the top half of the table.

As well as experienced England internationals
such as Alan Ball, Mick Channon and Kevin Keegan,
Southampton also had a strong academy system. Steve
Baker, Reuben Agboola and Danny Wallace had all
recently risen from the youth team to the first team,
and there were plenty more waiting to follow in their
footsteps.

In Gareth's age group, there were lots of talented
potential in the future Southampton stars, including a
defender called Jeff Kenna and, most impressive of all,
a striker called Alan Shearer, who scored goal after goal
after goal.

'Wow, these guys are *really* good!' Gareth realised
very quickly during his first training session. This
wasn't a casual kickaround in the school playground
in Crawley anymore; this was serious football against
seriously talented footballers. The Southampton scouts
searched far and wide to find the best young players.
Alan was from Newcastle in the north, while Jeff had
come all the way from Ireland.

Gareth knew that he had a lot of catching up to do,

but he didn't let it get him down. Challenge accepted! If he tried his hardest, hopefully he would reach the same level as the others eventually. Okay, so he would never be able to shoot as accurately and powerfully as Alan, or cross the ball like Jeff, but he focused on making the most of his own strengths: fitness, determination, and a fantastic football brain. For such a young midfielder, he could read the game really well, predicting what runs his opponents would make, and what they would do next once a pass arrived. That made it much easier for him to get into the right positions to win the ball back for his team.

'Well done, Gareth – great work!'

For the next two years, he did everything possible to prove he was good enough to be a Southampton player. He was a model student who never missed a training session, listened carefully to every word of advice from his coaches, and learned quickly from any mistakes.

Unfortunately, however, there was one thing that Gareth couldn't do anything about – his height. While the other players around him in his age group got taller and taller, he stayed skinny and small. In the early years, it hadn't mattered so much, but by the time he turned thirteen, his size was becoming a real problem on the pitch. As hard as he fought and as cleverly as he thought, he was still struggling to win the midfield battle against bigger, stronger opponents.

'Unlucky, Gareth, keep going!'

He carried on hoping and waiting for his growth spurt to come, and then one day, he received a letter in the post from Southampton's Head of Youth Development. It contained bad news, really bad news. It was the nightmare that every young footballer feared – Gareth was being released. The coaches had decided that he wasn't good enough, or big enough, to carry on playing for the club.

As Gareth stared down at the piece of paper in his hands, his eyes filled with tears. Rejection – it was a crushing blow, like a painful punch to the gut. For over two years, he had been working hard towards his professional football dream. He had given his all in training every week and watched the Southampton first team, thinking, 'I could be joining them someday soon!' But now, in one short letter, that dream had come to an end.

At first, Gareth thought about giving up on football completely – but no, he loved his favourite sport too much for that.

CHAPTER 4

BOUNCING BACK AT PALACE

Once the shock and hurt of his Southampton rejection had faded, Gareth began to think about other football options. He was still playing for his school team and for his county, but he also started playing for a Sunday league team in south-east London, where a lot of the boys trained with their biggest local professional club, Crystal Palace.

Would Gareth be good enough to get an opportunity there too? Yes, it looked that way. While Southampton were up in the First Division, Palace were down in the Second Division. But the more important question was: was he ready to give it another go at a higher level?

Yes, definitely! Gareth was desperate to prove Southampton wrong and to prove that he could still be a professional footballer. So eventually, he joined his teammates at the Palace training sessions and worked hard to show off his strengths straight away: fitness, determination, and a fantastic football brain. Loud and flashy really wasn't Gareth's style, but instead he calmly controlled the game from central midfield.

Block! Gareth bravely threw himself in front of the ball as an opponent was just about to shoot.

Interception! He guessed where the pass was going and got himself in the right position to get to the ball first.

Tackle! He waited patiently until the perfect moment to make the challenge.

Pass! He looked up, spotted a teammate in space, and played the ball to him quickly and accurately to launch another attack.

Goal! He burst forward into the box like his hero Bryan Robson and jumped high to head the cross in.

'Wow, we could really use a leader like him!' So what if the boy was still quite small and skinny for his age? The Palace youth coaches were so impressed that they invited Gareth to join the club's Under-18s, even though he was still only fifteen.

Hurray, he was back! Gareth was so glad that he hadn't given up on his football dream because now he was playing at a professional club again. There was no time to relax and enjoy his proud achievement, though; no – in order to stay and succeed, he was going to have to keep impressing and improving every week.

Just like at Southampton, the Palace youth team was packed with talented players. The stand-out stars were a speedy winger called John Salako and a smart defender called Richard Shaw. They were both a bit older than Gareth, but was he good enough to follow them into the first team one day? All he could do was work hard and hope for the best.

Gareth loved his first year at Palace, and at the end of it, he was given a difficult decision to make – stay at school, or focus fully on football? After getting good grades in his GCSEs, Gareth's teachers were encouraging him to continue his education at A level. But at the same time, Palace were offering him an apprenticeship, which meant he would be earning a small wage – plus they would pay the cost of his travel from his home in West Sussex every day.

So, which path would Gareth choose? Football, of course! While he liked studying and learning new things, this was a golden opportunity to follow his dream, and after his painful experience at Southampton, he couldn't say no to a second chance at Palace.

Aged sixteen, Gareth eagerly accepted his apprenticeship at the club. He couldn't wait to work his way up through the youth team, then the Reserves, until he finally became a Palace first-team player. When he said it like that, the path sounded straightforward, but it wasn't going to be easy at all – as he was about to find out.

CHAPTER 5

THE RIGHT FIT FOR PROFESSIONAL FOOTBALL?

'Noooooooooo!' Gareth groaned sleepily, reaching out to press the 'Snooze' button on his alarm clock. He gave himself five more minutes in bed, before he really had to get up if he was going to make it to the Palace training ground on time. He had to take two trains to get there, and what if one of them was running late?

Although Gareth was now living his professional football dream, so far it didn't feel like much fun at all. As a Palace apprentice, his days were long, dull and exhausting. At the end of each tough training session, he was then expected to help out around the place, cleaning the dressing room, the boots of the senior players, and even the toilets. Yuck, perhaps he should have stayed at school, after all!

It might have been more fun if Gareth had been surrounded by friends, but instead, he was struggling to fit in. In the dressing room, the other Palace players were all so loud and confident, whereas he was the quiet, shy kid sitting in the corner. It was the same problem out on the pitch too. The other young footballers around him were so strong and aggressive, and Gareth found it hard to compete. With the pressure on, he was making more and more mistakes and when he tried extra hard to fix them, he kept getting annoying little injuries all the time.

'Maybe I'm just not cut out for this,' he thought to himself as he hobbled off once again.

As the season went on, the doubts in Gareth's head grew bigger and bigger. Was this really what he wanted to do with his life? Was he the right fit for professional football? Then, just when he was ready to give up, his manager, Alan Smith, called him into his office.

'As a footballer, you've got no chance,' he said honestly. 'If I were you, I'd think about becoming a travel agent.'

At first, it was like that Southampton letter all over again. Gareth felt a crushing blow, a painful punch to the gut, and as he left the room, the tears were streaming down his face. But the next day, he realised that this time, there was one big difference. He hadn't been released; there was still a chance to turn things around. So instead of seeing Smith's words as the end of his football dream, he decided to take them as a challenge to prove his manager wrong.

Challenge accepted! After his bad experience at Southampton, Gareth had bounced back stronger than ever at Palace. Now, he was going to have to show his mental strength again. If he wanted to become a professional footballer, it was time for him to grow up and toughen up. To make it to the top, he was going to need more than just intelligence. He was going to need to be:

More confident,

More competitive,

More dedicated,

And even more eager to learn and improve.

'I can do this,' Gareth told himself, with a new fire

in his eyes. Day by day, game by game, he worked hard to change his manager's mind. At last, he grew taller and stronger, which added an extra edge to his game. Now, he was capable of playing in both defence and midfield, thanks to his fantastic football brain.

'I'm glad you didn't take my advice and become a travel agent!' Smith said with a smile.

Eventually, after a lot of time and effort, Gareth made it through the youth teams to the Reserves and then from the Reserves to training with the Palace first-team squad. The next step, however, was the hardest of all. Under manager Steve Coppell, 'The Eagles' were now flying high in the First Division and they had just reached the 1990 FA Cup final. Their first XI was packed with top-quality players, from Nigel Martyn in goal all the way through to Ian Wright and Mark Bright up front. So, how was Gareth going to break into the team?

The answer was: 'slowly'. To begin with, Gareth came on as a sub in the League Cup Second Round against Southend United in September 1990, and then six months later, he played in the Full Members'

Cup against Norwich City. Those were good games for giving young players a first taste of professional football, but nothing could prepare him for his next match: Liverpool away.

Yes, Gareth was going to make his league debut against the reigning First Division champions, and at Anfield, in front of over 35,000 jeering Liverpool fans. Not only that, but with Eric Young and Andy Thorn both out, Gareth would be playing in defence for Palace, against John Barnes, Peter Beardsley, and Ian Rush, three of the best forwards in world football.

Come on, Palace!

The fans feared that their young centre-back might get bullied by the big boys, but Gareth was up for the fight. Early on, he gave Rush a late kick in the back of the leg, sending him flying to the floor. *Yellow card!* After that, he did his best to stay calm and use his fantastic football brain instead. As the ball bounced down in the Palace box, Rush looked certain to score, but no, the new Palace Number 5 somehow stretched out his long right leg to make a brilliant block.

'Great defending, Gareth!' Nigel cheered, clapping

his goalkeeper gloves together.

But just when it looked like Palace might make it to half-time without conceding a goal, Liverpool took the lead. As the ball was played forward towards Rush, Gareth raced in to try and intercept the pass, but he ended up flat on the grass instead. By the time he was back on his feet and chasing back, Rush had played a one-two with Beardsley and fired a shot into the corner of the net. *1–0!*

'Noooooooo!' Gareth groaned, raising his face to the sky. Why hadn't he waited before making a tackle?

Gareth was going to have to learn fast in the First Division, but at least he was a proper professional footballer now.

CHAPTER 6

A PREMIER LEAGUE PLAYER: PART I

That loss to Liverpool was Gareth's one and only league appearance of the 1990–91 season, but he got lots more game-time in 1991–92. By then, he was a year older and wiser, and although he still wasn't yet a regular starter for Palace, he was now the next in line if anyone else couldn't play.

When John Humphrey hurt himself against Arsenal, it was Gareth who replaced him at right-back.

When Eric Young got an injury against QPR, it was Gareth who came on at centre-back.

And when Palace were missing both Andy Gray and Geoff Thomas, it was Gareth who moved into central midfield.

What a useful footballer he was! With his fantastic football brain, he could play almost anywhere on the pitch. In total, Gareth played in twenty-five games as Palace finished tenth in the table. Phew, they were staying in England's top division, which was about to get a multimillion-pound makeover, as well as a fancy new name: the Premier League.

'It's a whole new ball game,' said the advert on Sky Sports TV.

Gareth couldn't wait to be a part of the Premier League. It all seemed so stylish and exciting, and the timing was perfect because he had just earned his place in the Palace starting line-up at last, at the age of twenty-two. Andy Gray and Alan Pardew had both left the club during the summer, creating a gap in central midfield. Hurray! It was great news for Gareth but what about for the team? While Palace were busy selling their star players like Andy and Mark Bright, their first opponents of the season, Blackburn, had been busy buying lots of new players, including Gareth's old Southampton youth teammate, Alan Shearer, for a record £3.6 million.

That made Blackburn the clear favourites to win the match, but after sixty minutes, the score was still 1–1 and it was Palace on the attack. John Salako raced up the wing and won a corner-kick for his team. When Chris Coleman curled the ball into the box, the Blackburn keeper Bobby Mimms jumped up and punched it away, but only as far as the edge of the box, where Gareth was waiting. What a chance to make an instant impact in the Premier League! As the ball dropped and the Blackburn defenders rushed out to close him down, Gareth calmly made room to shoot with his right foot, steadied himself, and then BANG! He struck it sweetly, sending it flying over the heads of all the players, including the goalkeeper, and into the top corner. *2–1!*

Gooooooooooooooooooooaaaaaaaaaaaaaaaalllllllllllllll lllllllllll!!!!!!!!!!!!!!!!!!!

Gareth had scored his first senior goal on his Premier League debut! By the time his amazing achievement had sunk in, he was at the bottom of a big pile of celebrating Palace players.

Yesssssssss, Gaz!

What a strike!

Nice one, mate, I didn't know you could shoot like that!

Unfortunately, the game ended in a 3–3 draw, and there were lots more frustrating moments to come for Palace. Out of their first seventeen Premier League matches, they only managed to win one. Uh-oh – they were bottom of the league and in real relegation trouble.

Gareth wasn't giving up, though; he was ready to give his all to save his team. Despite being a young player in his first full season, he was already becoming one of Palace's leaders on the pitch. Against Sheffield United, he charged in to win the ball in midfield, dribbled forward and fired another unstoppable shot into the top corner. *2–0!*

Gooooooooooooooooooooaaaaaaaaaaaaaaallllllllllllll llllllllllllll!!!!!!!!!!!!!!!!!!!

'Come onnnnn!' Gareth roared with passion as he jumped into Mark Bright's arms. That important goal and victory lifted Palace off the bottom of the Premier League table and it led to a run of five wins in a row.

'We are staying up, I said we are staying up!' the supporters suddenly began to sing.

Gareth continued his good form by scoring against Nottingham Forest and setting another one up for new striker Chris Armstrong against Chelsea. Both games, however, finished 1–1, and draws weren't going to be enough to keep Palace in the Premier League. They needed wins, and with Gareth controlling the midfield battle, they managed to pick up the maximum six points against Middlesbrough and Ipswich.

We are staying up, I said we are staying up!

Ahead of the final day of the season, Palace sat one place above the relegation zone, and three points above their nearest rivals, Oldham Athletic. That meant that if The Eagles could avoid defeat in their last game away at Arsenal, then they would be staying in the Premier League for another season. But if they lost and Oldham beat Southampton, then Palace would be the ones going down instead.

What football drama! Gareth had never felt so nervous as he walked out for kick-off that day. Could he help keep his club up? All he could do was his best.

At half-time, the scores were:

Arsenal 1 Palace 0 (goal scored by Ian Wright, against his old club)

And

Oldham 2 Southampton 1.

Uh-oh – it didn't look good for Gareth and his teammates, and it got even worse early in the second half when Oldham scored two more goals to lead 4–1. Now, Palace desperately needed to get an equaliser, but as they pushed forward on the attack, Arsenal punished them twice. *2–0, then 3–0!*

As he watched the ball bobble agonisingly across the penalty area and into the Palace net for the third time, Gareth turned away and threw his hands to his head in horror. It was over; despite all his hard work, his team were going down.

In that heartbreaking moment, it felt like the end of everything – his Premier League dream and his England dream too. But it wasn't long before Gareth was thinking positively about how to get Palace promoted again.

CHAPTER 7

CAPTAIN COMEBACK

That summer, there were a series of major changes at Crystal Palace as the club prepared for life in the Championship. Out went their manager Steve Coppell, experienced midfielder Eddie McGoldrick, and captain Geoff Thomas.

The new man in charge was Gareth's old youth team coach, Alan Smith, and one of his first tasks was to choose a new Palace skipper. Who should it be – one of the more experienced members of the team like Nigel Martyn or Eric Young? No, there was another player who Smith already knew well, and who he believed was born to be a leader: Gareth! So, at the age of only twenty-three, he was given the captain's armband to wear.

Wow, what an honour! Gareth felt really proud, but also a little worried at first. He was still just starting out as a professional footballer – was he ready for the extra responsibility? Plus, some of his Palace teammates were a lot older than him – wouldn't it be weird if he tried to tell them what to do? No, despite his doubts, Gareth was determined to prove himself and lead Palace back to the Premier League.

'Come on, we can do this!' he urged his teammates as they kicked off their 1993–94 season. The Eagles began with a draw and a defeat, but they soon found their form after that. Eric and Chris Coleman stayed solid at the back, Chris Armstrong looked lethal in attack, and in the middle, there was Gareth, calmly bringing the whole team together. Although he wasn't the loudest player on the pitch, he always led by example with his remarkable work-rate, and he wasn't afraid to raise his voice if he really needed to.

Not good enough, lads. Wake up, we've got work to do in the second half!

As a box-to-box midfielder, Gareth was getting

better and better. On top of making lots of tackles and interceptions for Palace, he was also grabbing goals and assists.

Against Portsmouth, Gareth showed off both sides of his game in one brilliant move. After stealing the ball back in his own half, he weaved his way past one tackle, and then dribbled forward at full speed. He looked up for teammates to pass to, but as the defenders backed away, he decided to shoot from long distance instead. *BANG!* He sent the ball flying through the air and into the corner of the net.

Goooooooooooooooooooooaaaaaaaaaaaaaaaaaalllllllllllllll llllllllllll!!!!!!!!!!!!!!!!!!!

It was the greatest goal that Gareth had ever scored, and before he knew it, he was at the bottom of a big pile of Palace players again.

'Nice one, Skip!'

After his wondergoal, Gareth felt full of confidence, and suddenly he couldn't stop scoring:

A bursting run against West Brom,

A quick-reaction rebound against Stoke City,

A clever flick-on against Grimsby,

A calm finish against Watford,

A brave header against Birmingham City...

When their captain scored, Palace always seemed to win, and so by February 1994, they were clear at the top of the Championship table. With each victory, they were getting closer and closer to an instant return to the Premier League.

Crystal Palace 1 Millwall 0,

Luton Town 0 Crystal Palace 1,

Crystal Palace 1 Barnsley 0...

Hurray, it was official: they had been promoted back up to the Premier League! For Palace, the season wasn't over yet, though. If they could win one more match against Middlesbrough, they would also win the league title.

In the first half, The Eagles found themselves 1–0 down, but they fought back brilliantly, and who inspired the comeback? Their captain, of course! With a clever flick header, Gareth guided the ball into the net for the ninth time that season. *1–1!*

Goooooooooooooooooooaaaaaaaaaaaaaaaallllllllllllll llllllllllll!!!!!!!!!!!!!!!!!!

As always, the Palace players listened to their popular young leader. David Whyte scored the second goal and then Chris Armstrong headed in a third, which turned out to be the matchwinner.

'Yessssssss!' As the final whistle blew, Gareth punched the air with passion and pride, and then jogged around the pitch, giving hugs and high-fives to his teammates. All that hard work had been worth it because now the league title was theirs. What an incredible comeback – twelve months after the misery of relegation, they were returning to the Premier League as Champions!

But before that, Palace had one more game to go and it was back home at Selhurst Park, the perfect place for a big promotion party. When the team arrived at the stadium, they found thousands of fans already waiting to welcome their heroes.

And it's Crystal Palace,
Crystal Palace FC,
We're by far the greatest team,
The world has ever seen!

What an amazing atmosphere! The stands were covered in red and blue shirts, scarves and balloons, and before kick-off, the Palace players warmed up wearing special T-shirts that said 'CHAMPIONS' on the front and 'WE TOLD YOU SO' on the back. Then one by one, they went up to collect their league winners' medals: Nigel, Eric, Dean, David, Chris Coleman, Chris Armstrong, Richard Shaw, John Salako, Simon Rodger...

...And finally, Gareth! As the captain, he was handed the shiny league trophy as well as his winner's medal. He stood there in the centre of the pitch posing for photos, until the other players grew impatient.

Lift it up, man, lift it up!

So Gareth did as he was told, raising the trophy high above his head with a huge smile on his face.

Hurraaaaaaaaaaaaaaaaaaaayyyyyyyyyyyy!!!!!!!!!

It had been a superb season for all the Palace players, but especially for Gareth, who hadn't missed a single match. Even with the extra responsibility of wearing the captain's armband, he had still managed to raise his game to the next level. Now, he couldn't wait to prove himself as a top Premier League player.

CHAPTER 8

A PREMIER LEAGUE PLAYER: PART II

Gareth was really hoping that his second experience as a Premier League player would be a lot less painful, but the early signs didn't look good. Palace had started the 1994–95 season by losing 6–1 to Liverpool, and now with a few minutes to go away at Aston Villa, they were facing defeat again.

'Come on, keep going!' Gareth shouted, urging his teammates on. He refused to give up; there was still time for them to get an equaliser.

As one last long ball sailed into the crowded Villa penalty area, Gareth made a late run into the box, completely unmarked. His chances of scoring were low, but if Chris Armstrong could win the header...

FLICK!

…Gareth was in luck! As the ball dropped down, he rushed towards it and then steadied himself to strike it first time. He just had to stay calm and finish, like he had done so many times in the Championship the previous year. With a swing of his right foot, he sent the ball flying past the Villa keeper. *1–1!*

Goooooooooooooooooooaaaaaaaaaaaaaaaaaallllllllllllll llllllllllll!!!!!!!!!!!!!!!!!!

After watching the ball land safely in the net, Gareth threw his arms up in the air and waited for his teammates to join him. Another game, another crucial, captain's goal! No, Palace hadn't won the match, but in their battle to stay in the Premier League, one point was definitely better than none.

Loss, draw, draw, loss… It took eight games, but eventually, the Eagles got their first win of the season away at Arsenal. At the final whistle, Gareth roared with relief; at last, their bad run was over.

'Right, now we've got to keep on winning!' he told his delighted teammates in the dressing room.

Yessssssssssss!

Everton, Leicester City, Coventry City, Ipswich Town – Palace beat them all as they climbed up into the top half of the Premier League table. The Eagles were flying high in the League Cup too. In the Fourth Round, they thrashed Aston Villa 4–1, thanks to another incredible display by their captain.

First, Gareth made a late burst into the box to sweep Chris Armstrong's cross into the net. *2–1!*

Goooooooooooooooooooooaaaaaaaaaaaaaaaaallllllllllllll llllllllllll!!!!!!!!!!!!!!!!!!!

'Get in, Gaz!' John cheered as he lifted the Palace leader up into the air.

Then moments later, Gareth calmly fired the ball into the bottom corner again. *3–1!*

Yessssssssss! Dean was the first to throw his arms around his captain, followed by the two Chrises, Coleman and Armstrong. The Palace players were working so well together as a team, and in the next round they thumped Manchester City 4–0 to make it through to the semi-final. In fact, they made it to the semi-finals of the League Cup and the FA Cup that season, where they lost to, respectively, Liverpool and

Manchester United.

While the cup runs were fun, staying in the Premier League was Palace's priority, and unfortunately, things were starting to go wrong there. Although they stayed strong in defence, the team failed to score a single league goal, from November all the way through to January. *0–0, 0–0, 0–1, 0–1...* with each frustrating draw or defeat, they slipped further and further down the table until they found themselves falling into the relegation zone.

Uh-oh, not again! Gareth was desperate to stop his club from going down, but what could he do to help turn things around? He scored a late equaliser against Manchester United and then led his team to another victory over Ipswich. Those four extra points moved Palace up to sixteenth place. Phew, that was more like it!

Unfortunately, however, their good form didn't last long, and The Eagles only managed to win three of their last fifteen matches. On the final day of the season, they needed to beat Newcastle to stand any chance of staying up, but by half-time, they were already 3–0 down. They managed to fight back in the second half to make it 3–2, but that wasn't enough. Despite Gareth's best efforts, Palace were going straight back down to the Championship again.

It was a sad end to a very strange season for the club. They had reached the semi-finals of both cup competitions, but they had also been relegated from the Premier League. Now, the big question was – would Palace be able to keep hold of their best players? Sadly, the answer was no. That summer:

John and Richard signed for Coventry City,

Chris Coleman was bought by Blackburn,

Chris Armstrong transferred to Tottenham,

Eric went to Wolves…

…And what about Gareth? Although he was proud to be the Palace captain, he really didn't want to go down again. He had proved himself in the Premier League, and he believed that was where he belonged. Plus, he hadn't yet given up on his dream of playing for England one day, and he would be turning twenty-five soon…

In June 1995, Gareth got an offer from Aston Villa.

Although they had only finished one place above Palace the previous season, Villa were a bigger football club with much higher ambitions for the future. They had already spent £3.5 million on new striker Savo Miloševic to partner Dwight Yorke up front, and now they were willing to pay £2.5 million to sign Gareth too.

After ten unforgettable years at Palace, full of highs and lows, it was finally time for him to move on. 'It was a difficult decision to leave,' Gareth explained as he waved goodbye to the fans, 'but I felt I needed a new challenge.'

CHAPTER 9

VILLA'S BRILLIANT BACK THREE

For Gareth, it turned out to be a case of new club, new position. Aston Villa already had three excellent central midfielders – Ian Taylor, Mark Draper and captain Andy Townsend – as well as exciting youngsters like Lee Hendrie and Riccardo Scimeca coming through.

So instead of controlling the midfield, the Villa manager Brian Little asked Gareth to use his leadership skills and his fantastic football brain in a deeper role in defence, as he'd done in his younger years at Palace. Little liked his team to play with a back three, and he believed that Gareth would be the perfect fit for the left side, alongside the skill and experience of Paul McGrath and the strength and speed of Ugo Ehiogu.

Challenge accepted! Gareth was determined to adapt to a different role as well as a different style of football. Whereas at Palace, the defenders were told to boot the ball high and long towards the strikers, at Villa, they were encouraged to take their time and move it around more carefully from back to front. That really suited a smart thinker like Gareth, and thanks to his days in central midfield, his passing had improved a lot.

From the very start, Villa's three defenders formed a brilliant partnership together. In the first game of the 1995–96 Premier League season, there was no way through for Manchester United's forwards, Paul Scholes and Brian McClair. If they managed to get past the first defender, one of the others came across to deal with the danger.

'Cheers, Paul!'

And if they somehow got past all three, then they still had to beat Mark Bosnich in goal.

'Great save, Bozzy!'

Villa looked so calm and organised at the back, and they looked dangerous in attack too. Ian slid in to score their first goal, Mark fired in the second, and Dwight added a third from the penalty spot. Wow, 3–0 – the Villa fans were in dreamland! Eventually, United did manage to pull one goal back, but there was nothing the Villa defence could do to stop David Beckham's swerving, long-range shot. Oh well, a 3–1 win was still a great start to the season, especially against Manchester United.

As he walked around the pitch after the final whistle, clapping his new club's fans, Gareth was very glad that he'd said yes to Aston Villa. He knew that he still had lots to learn about defending at the highest level, but he was in the best possible place to develop and improve. Paul was a player who he had admired for a long time, ever since his days at Manchester United, and Ugo was one of the best young defenders in Britain. Gareth already felt so comfortable alongside the two of them; it was as if they had been playing together for years.

Manchester United weren't the only team who struggled against Villa's brilliant back three that season. In their first eleven games, they kept five cleansheets, against Tottenham, Bolton, Wimbledon, Coventry, and Everton. At the end of the season, they had one of the best records in the whole division – just thirty-five goals conceded in thirty-eight games.

'Look what a difference a top defender makes!'
Gareth joked with Ugo and Paul.

Villa finished fourth in the Premier League, which
meant they qualified for the UEFA Cup. And that wasn't
all – in February, they also beat Arsenal to reach the
League Cup final. After Dwight grabbed two away
goals in the first leg at Highbury, it was time for Villa's
defenders to shine in the second. They just had to hold
on and claim a cleansheet at home, and that's exactly
what they did. Arsenal's attackers tried and tried, but
they couldn't break through the brilliant Villa back three.

From the right wing, Paul Merson tried to cross the
ball into the box, but Gareth was there to block it.

Lee Dixon launched the ball forward towards Ian
Wright, but Ugo got there first to head it away.

Ray Parlour played a throughball for Wright to chase,
but Paul used his speed and strength to win the race.

With seconds to go, Dennis Bergkamp got the ball
on the edge of the box and tried to turn, but in came
Gareth to win it back with another perfectly timed
tackle.

'Hurraaaaaaaay!' cheered the 40,000 fans at Villa Park. That was it; their team was on their way to Wembley! The players raced around hugging each other and the supporters stormed onto the pitch to celebrate with them.

What a night, and hopefully there would be an even better one to follow once they won the League Cup final. There, Villa faced Leeds United and their new star striker, Tony Yeboah. The Ghanaian was quick and powerful and he could score goals from anywhere. So, could the brilliant Villa back three mark him out of the game? Of course they could!

Gary Kelly tried to reach Yeboah with a long pass, but Gareth saw it coming and cut it out.

Yeboah chested the ball down, but by the time it bounced, Paul was there to steal it off him.

Yeboah jumped up for a header, but he had no chance against Ugo.

Villa looked so calm and organised at the back, and they looked dangerous in attack too.

Savo Miloševic dribbled forward and unleashed a sensational strike that sailed into the top corner. *1–0!*

A clearance fell straight to Ian, who volleyed the ball

into the bottom corner. *2–0!*

After that, Leeds brought on Brian Deane and Tomas Brolin to try and change the game, but it didn't work. The Villa defence dealt with every dribble, cross and shot. Then in the eighty-eighth minute, Mark set up Savo, who laid the ball across to Dwight. *3–0!*

Game over – Villa were the 1996 League Cup winners! Gareth waited for the final whistle to blow and then punched the air with both fists. What a feeling! In his first season at his new club, he had helped them to win a major cup. As the players climbed the steps for the trophy presentation, Gareth couldn't help smiling and high-fiving all the Villa fans he passed. Once the heavy cup was safely in Andy's hands, he lifted it high above his head and Wembley went wild.

Hurraaaaaaaay!

The Villa celebrations continued down on the pitch. The trophy passed from player to player until eventually Gareth and Ugo stood together, each holding one handle of the League Cup. What a wonderful defensive duo they were. It wouldn't be long before they were playing together for England too.

CHAPTER 10

EURO 96: ENGLAND DREAM COME TRUE

Just three days after lifting the League Cup, Gareth
was back at Wembley, living his England dream at last.
He had made his international debut a few months
earlier as a second-half substitute, but this time,
against Bulgaria, he was in the starting line-up.

How exciting! Gareth couldn't wait for kick-
off. Although the match was only a friendly, it was
a massive chance to impress the manager, Terry
Venables, especially with Euro 96 coming up in the
summer. Tony Adams would be one of England's
centre-backs at the tournament, but who would the
other be? Sol Campbell? Steve Howey? No, Gareth,
hopefully! He had worked so hard for his opportunity;

now, he just had to stay calm and defend like he did at Villa.

In the end, he didn't have that much defending to do as England beat Bulgaria 1–0, but the main thing was that Gareth hadn't conceded any goals, and the cleansheets continued:

England 3 Hungary 0,

China 0 England 3...

The China match was extra special for Gareth because for the last fifteen minutes, he got to play alongside his Villa partner Ugo, who was making his England debut. Would they get to play together at Euro 96 too?

On 28 May, Venables announced his twenty-two-man squad for the tournament, which included the names 'Adams', 'Campbell', 'Howey', and 'Southgate', but sadly not 'Ehiogu'. While he felt sorry for his friend, Gareth was delighted and honoured to make the list himself. He had come a long way from rejection at Southampton and relegation at Crystal Palace.

All across the country, the buzz was building. For

the first time since winning the World Cup in 1966, England was hosting a major tournament. Was football finally coming home again? That's what the supporters were hoping for as the Three Lions kicked things off against Switzerland. As well as home advantage, they also had their strongest team for years:

Teddy Sheringham and Alan Shearer up front,

Steve McManaman, Darren Anderton, Paul Gascoigne and Paul Ince in midfield,

And in defence, Stuart Pearce, Gary Neville, Tony Adams and…Gareth!

Yes, all of Gareth's hard work had paid off because Venables had picked him to start at centre-back ahead of Sol and Steve. Walking out at Wembley was the latest proudest moment of Gareth's life, but he knew that to keep his place, he was going to have to put in a solid performance.

The Three Lions started the match well and midway through the first half, Wembley erupted as Alan gave them the lead with a powerful strike. What a relief – England were up and running at Euro 96 already!

Now, could the defence do their job and secure the victory? With ten minutes to go, Gareth went to head the ball away from danger, but he stumbled and ended up heading it back into the England box by mistake. Uh-oh! It landed at the feet of Swiss striker Marco Grassi, whose shot flicked off Stuart's raised arm. Handball! Penalty!

'No way!' Gareth shouted, swiping angrily at the air. He was furious with the referee's decision, but also with himself. After all, it was his fault that the ball was in the box in the first place. There was nothing he could do about it now, though, as Kubilay Türkyilmaz stepped up for Switzerland and… sent David Seaman the wrong way. *1–1!*

A draw was a very disappointing result for England, and it meant that their next group game against local rivals Scotland was now a must-win match. Despite that poorly placed header, Gareth got to stay in the starting line-up, and he was determined not to make any more mistakes. In the first half, he bravely blocked a dangerous shot from Gary McAllister and won his battle in the air against Scotland's superstar striker

Gordon Durie.

At half-time, the score was still 0–0, but early in the second half, Gary raced up the right wing and delivered a great cross for Alan to score again. 1–0!

'Yesssssss!' Gareth cheered, throwing his arms up in delight.

Right, could England keep their concentration and their lead this time? In the seventy-eighth minute, it looked like it was going to be Switzerland all over again. As Stuart McCall crossed the ball into the box, Tony slid in and fouled Durie. *Penalty!*

'Noooooo, not again!' Gareth thought to himself as he threw his head back in disbelief.

McAllister stepped up for Scotland and… David made a super save!

Phew, England were still winning! After saying a quick thanks to his keeper, Gareth got back to work, organising his teammates to face the corner-kick. 'Come on, focus!'

A minute later, Seaman launched a goal-kick towards Teddy, who laid it off to Darren, who lifted a ball over the top to Gazza. With his first touch, he flicked the ball over Colin Hendry's head and with his second, he volleyed it in. *2–0!*

What a goal to win the game for England! At the final whistle, Gareth turned to the fans and lifted both arms up in the air. Job done; now, if they could beat the Netherlands, they would top the group.

The match was expected to be their toughest test so far, but the Three Lions made it look easy. Under Venables, their team spirit was stronger than ever and they were determined to win together. Gareth marked Dennis Bergkamp out of the game, just like he had for Villa against Arsenal, and at the other end, England's forwards tore the Dutch defence apart.

Alan scored from the penalty spot. *1–0!*

Teddy made it two with a terrific header. *2–0!*

Alan blasted the ball into the net again. *3–0!*

Darren's shot was saved, but the rebound fell to Teddy. *4–0!*

Wow, suddenly England were on fire at Euro 96! The only disappointment was that the defence couldn't keep their second cleansheet of the tournament. With time running out, Bergkamp flicked a clever ball through to Kluivert, who sped past Gareth and slipped the ball through David's legs. *4–1!*

Never mind – the main thing was that the Three Lions were through to the quarter-finals. There, they faced Spain, one of the best teams at the tournament. After thrashing the Netherlands, the England fans expected goals, but unfortunately, none arrived, even after thirty minutes of extra-time. The game was going to… PENALTIES!

The atmosphere at Wembley Stadium grew tenser and tenser. England had lost their only other major shoot-out, against West Germany at the 1990 World Cup. Could they do better this time, with the home fans cheering them on? As the tired players huddled together, Venables asked for volunteers. Alan said yes, and so did David Platt, Stuart, Gazza and Robbie Fowler.

'Good luck!' Gareth told each of England's first five brave penalty takers. Then, with his heart beating fast, he stood with the rest of his teammates on the halfway line to watch the drama unfold.

Alan showed the way with a confident spot-kick,

and their next three players all found the net too.
Four out of four! Fernando Hierro had already missed
one for Spain, which meant that Miguel Nadal had
to score, or his team was out. Up he stepped and…
David made another super save!

With adrenaline rushing through his body, Gareth
raced over to hug England's penalty hero and join the
joyful team celebrations. Hurray, they had won the
shoot-out and they were into the Euro 96 semi-finals!

CHAPTER 11

EURO 96:
PENALTY PAIN

26 June 1996, Wembley Stadium

Football – was it finally coming home? That's what
people were saying and singing all over England. As
Gareth and his teammates travelled from their hotel in
Hertfordshire to Wembley Stadium, the streets were lined
with fans waving flags and wishing them good luck.

Come on, England!

Wow – football fever had completely taken over
the country because their national team was now only
one win away from reaching the Euro 96 final. To get
there, however, the Three Lions would have to do
something they hadn't done at a major tournament

since 1966 – beat their old rivals, Germany.

Come on, England!

For the big game, Venables decided to switch his defence from a back four to a back three. That was no problem at all for Gareth because it was the formation he was used to playing at Aston Villa. Just instead of Paul and Ugo, he would have Tony and Stuart alongside him.

'Let's do this!' they cheered together as they took up their positions on the pitch.

With the Wembley crowd roaring them on, England raced off to the best possible start. In the third minute of the match, Gazza curled in a corner, Tony got a flick-on at the near post, and Alan headed the ball in. *1–0!*

Yesssssssssssss!

England were in dreamland, but once again, they failed to hold on to their lead. Less than fifteen minutes later, Germany's striker Stefan Kuntz slid in ahead of Stuart to score the equaliser. *1–1!*

After such an exciting start, the Euro 96 semi-final calmed down and became a cagey battle, where both teams were desperate to avoid making mistakes. There

was no winning goal after ninety minutes, and there
was no winning goal after 120 minutes either, despite
England's best efforts in extra-time. First, Darren's
shot bounced back off the post, and then Gazza came
agonisingly close to reaching Alan's cross.

Noooooooooooo!

The game was going to... PENALTIES!

England were feeling more confident after their
success against Spain, and their first five takers all
stepped up and scored. But with Germany scoring
all of their spot-kicks too, the shoot-out went to...
SUDDEN DEATH!

'So, who's up next?' the nervous England fans
wondered.

Gulp, it was time for the moment that Gareth had
hoped would never happen. In the huddle, none of
his other teammates had volunteered – not Steve, not
Darren, not Paul, not Tony – and so he had agreed
to take England's sixth spot-kick. Gareth hadn't said
yes because he was good at taking penalties; in fact,
he had only taken one in his whole professional
career, and that one had hit the post. No, he had

said yes because he was a leader who liked to take responsibility. Even though it was only his ninth England cap, if his team needed him to step up, then he would do it.

But as he began the long walk forward from the halfway line, Gareth was regretting that brave decision. He felt the hopes of 48 million people resting heavily on his shoulders. What if he missed? What if England didn't reach the Euro 96 and it was all his fault?

'Come on, stay calm,' Gareth told himself as he placed the ball down on the penalty spot and then took a few steps back. But the nerves had taken over his body, and he no longer felt in control of his own legs.

As he waited for the referee's whistle, Gareth's full focus was on making good contact with the ball. As long as he hit the target, then he had a chance of scoring. What he hadn't really thought about, or practised in training, was:

a) Where exactly he wanted to place his penalty – *top corner, bottom corner, left, right, straight down the middle?*

b) How much power he should put on the ball –

not too much, as much as possible, somewhere in between?

Gareth ran up to the ball at speed, but his shot was more like a strong pass that slid across the grass... and straight to the German keeper. *Saved!*

NOOOOOOOOOOO!

Gareth felt that crushing blow again, like a painful punch to the gut. With his hands on his hips, he turned away and stared down at the ground in despair. His worst nightmare had come true. Taking long, deep breaths, he made his way back to the halfway line, but really, he just wanted to disappear. Instead, however, he was stuck in the middle of a football pitch, with millions of people watching him suffer and fail.

'Hey, don't worry about it – it could happen to anyone,' Stuart said, putting an arm around his shoulder. After missing one of England's spot-kicks in the 1990 World Cup semi-final, he knew exactly how Gareth was feeling. 'You were brave enough to step forward and you did your best.'

Plus, the semi-final wasn't over quite yet because to win, Germany still needed to score. David had another chance to be the England hero – could he save the day like he had against Spain? Andreas Möller stepped up and… fired a shot into the roof of the net.

Now, it really was all over. England's amazing Euro 96 adventure had come to an end.

Gareth's teammates did their best to comfort him as they walked off the pitch together, but in that moment, nothing could soothe his pain. They hadn't reached the Euro 96 and it was all his fault. It was the lowest point in his football career, and he felt like he had let so many people down with that penalty miss: the other England players, and the entire nation.

He spent the next few days staying away from the media spotlight, but Gareth couldn't hide from his own thoughts. Why hadn't he placed his shot properly in the corner? Or as his mum asked him on the phone, 'Why didn't you just belt it?'

Gareth had no answer for that, but there was nothing he could do about it now, except learn from his mistakes and bounce back stronger than ever. Despite all the cruel comments and newspaper headlines, there was no way he was giving up on his England dream.

CHAPTER 12

CAPTAIN CONSISTENT

Euro 96 was still fresh in everyone's minds as the new Premier League season kicked off in August. It wasn't always easy, but Gareth did his best to ignore any boos and insults from the away fans, and focused instead on putting that penalty miss behind him.

After losing at Sheffield Wednesday, Villa needed a victory in their second game against Blackburn. With sixty minutes gone, it was still 0–0, but the home team were on the attack. Eventually, the Blackburn defence managed to clear the danger away, but only as far as the edge of the box, where Gareth was waiting. With his first touch, he controlled the bouncing ball, and with his second, he sent it flying into the top corner. *1–0!*

Goooooooooooooooooooaaaaaaaaaaaaaaaaalllllllllllllll
lllllllllllll!!!!!!!!!!!!!!!!!!!!

What a strike and what a way to respond to all the
hurtful abuse! Gareth leapt into the air with a flying
right fist, as his teammates raced over to celebrate.
They knew what a hard time it had been for him and
they were so pleased to see him fighting back on the
football pitch.

'Well done, you deserved that, mate!' Ugo cheered
as they shared a hug.

Following Paul's move to Derby County, Villa's
brilliant back three had become a terrific back two,
but Gareth and Ugo worked so well together that
it didn't make much difference. They had a natural
understanding out on the pitch, but even so, they
never stopped talking to each other, telling the other
where to go and who to watch out for.

'I've got it, Ugo!'

'Gaz, that's your man!'

With their combination of pace, power, intelligence
and composure, they formed the perfect partnership,

capable of keeping the Premier League's best attackers quiet:

Aston Villa 0 Manchester United's David Beckham, Ryan Giggs, Eric Cantona and Andy Cole 0,

Aston Villa 1 Liverpool's Steve McManaman, John Barnes, Robbie Fowler and Stan Collymore 0.

'Yessssssssssssssss!' Gareth and Ugo yelled as they celebrated another excellent cleansheet together.

Villa's attackers weren't scoring a lot of goals, but luckily the team had the second-best defensive record in the Premier League – thirty-seven games played, thirty-four goals conceded. And with another 1–0 win over Southampton on the last day of the season, they secured a fifth-place finish in the Premier League to qualify for Europe.

'Come onnnnnnn!' Gareth roared with relief as the final whistle blew. He was really proud of the way he had bounced back from his England penalty miss. Even during the hardest year of his career, he had stayed so calm and consistent at the heart of the Villa defence.

That summer, when Andy moved to

Middlesbrough, Gareth was the obvious choice to take over the as Villa captain. He had worn the armband before at Palace, plus he had the full respect of his teammates, who already relied on his organisation.

So, could Gareth lead Villa to more glory during the 1997–98 season? Unfortunately, instead of climbing up the Premier League table, they found themselves slipping down. While rivals like Chelsea and Leeds United had made major improvements to their squads, Villa had only signed one new player: Stan Collymore for £7 million. That wasn't enough, and as a result, they were falling behind. In fact, after losing their first four games, they found themselves at the bottom of the league.

'Come on, we're so much better than this, boys!'

Despite Gareth's frustrations with the club, it was his job as captain to lift the team spirit and get Villa back to their best. It took time but eventually, the performances improved and they ended the season in style, winning ten of their last fourteen games, including impressive victories over Liverpool, Chelsea, West Ham and Arsenal.

'That's more like it, lads!' Gareth clapped and cheered. After a difficult start, they had done well to fight back and finish in seventh place.

Plus, Villa had also enjoyed a fun European adventure. In the UEFA Cup, they battled their way past French club Bordeaux, and then Spanish side Athletic Bilbao. The key to their success was their defence, and their captain in particular. In the one match Gareth missed, against Romanian club Steaua Bucharest, Villa lost 2–1 without their calm, consistent leader. But when he returned for the second leg, they won 2–0 to reach the UEFA Cup quarter-finals.

'It's great to have you back, Skip!' Ugo said with a smile.

Villa's next opponents were the Spanish giants, Atlético Madrid. Could Gareth and Ugo keep their star striker, Christian Vieri, quiet? The answer was yes for the first forty minutes, but just before half-time, Villa conceded a penalty, which Vieri fired home. 1–0!

'Keep going, guys!' Gareth urged his team on.

Even when Atlético scored again in the first half of

the second leg at Villa Park, he didn't give up. Gareth got the ball on the halfway line and played one of his perfect long passes to Lee Hendrie on the left, who cut the ball across to Dwight, who laid it back to Ian. *2–1!*

'Let's go, we can do this!' Gareth roared with conviction. The comeback was on and two minutes later, Lee set up Stan, who rocketed a shot into the top corner. *2–2!*

The Villa players started to run over to the fans to celebrate, until their captain called them back to the halfway line. Atlético were still ahead on away goals. 'Come on, we need to score one more!' Gareth yelled out to his team.

In the last ten minutes, Villa attacked and attacked, searching for a winner, but sadly, they were out of luck. As Gareth launched one last long ball forward, the referee blew the final whistle.

Unfortunately, Villa's UEFA Cup journey was over, but it had given Gareth a real taste for European travel. Hopefully, he would be going back to France that summer to play for England at the World Cup.

CHAPTER 13

1998, 2000:
MORE ENGLAND MISERY

Thankfully, Gareth's penalty miss had not spelled the end of his England career. After Euro 96, Glenn Hoddle had replaced Terry Venables as manager, but as the Three Lions kicked off their qualification campaign for the 1998 World Cup against Moldova, Gareth was still there at the heart of the defence. And there he stayed, so calm and so consistent, as England secured their place at the tournament in France.

Gareth couldn't wait for his World Cup dream to come true. He had grown up watching his hero Bryan Robson star at Spain 82 and Mexico 86, and now it was his turn to represent his country at the world's biggest football competition. Unbelievable! When he walked out onto the pitch in Marseille for England's opening match, it felt like one of the greatest and proudest moments of his life.

'Come onnnnnnn!' he roared with passion at the end of the national anthem.

Hoddle had picked Gareth, Tony and Sol together in the same defence, and the Tunisia strikers had no chance against such a formidable back three. At the other end, Alan and Paul Scholes scored the goals to fire the Three Lions to victory. Job done! England were off to an excellent start, but for their second game against Romania, the manager was forced to make a change: in came Gary Neville, and out went... Gareth.

Noooooooo!

Sadly, he had injured his ankle and so he would have to support his country from the subs bench instead.

Come on, England!

Unfortunately, however, they lost 2–1 without him. Gareth was hoping to be back fit in time to help his team in their crucial last group game against

Colombia, but no, in the end, he had to cheer them on from the sidelines again.

Come on, England!

It was a match they desperately needed to win, and they did, thanks to two great goals from Darren and David Beckham. Hurray, they were through to the Round of 16! There, they took on Argentina in one of the most exciting matches of the tournament:

Gabriel Batistuta scored from the penalty spot. *1–0!*

Four minutes later, so did Alan for England. *1–1!*

Michael Owen weaved his way through the Argentina defence to score a wondergoal. *2–1!*

Then Javier Zanetti equalised from a cleverly worked free kick. *2–2!*

Wow, what an action-packed first half, and there was more drama to come early in the second half. When Diego Simeone fouled him, David kicked out angrily at the Argentinian, who fell to the floor theatrically. The referee reached into his pocket and pulled out a… RED CARD!

No way! Watching from the bench, Gareth let out a big sigh – uh-oh, England were in big trouble now.

For the next twenty minutes, they battled on bravely with ten men, but as the players grew tired, Argentina pushed forward on the attack. It was time for Hoddle to make a substitution: off came left back Graeme Le Saux and on came… Gareth!

Right, now that his ankle had healed, he had some serious defending to do. This was his chance to step up for England and maybe even become a hero again.

With Gareth's calm presence at the back, The Three Lions managed to hold on until the final whistle, and then through thirty minutes of extra-time too. The game was going to… PENALTIES!

Noooooo, not again! This time, as the exhausted England players huddled together near the halfway line, Gareth didn't volunteer. He wasn't ready to go through penalty pain again. He could hardly bear to even watch the shoot-out.

So, who would be brave enough to take one for England? Alan would go first and score as usual, but who else? Two of their best options, David Beckham and Paul Scholes, had been sent off and subbed off, so instead, Hoddle turned to:

Paul Ince… *Saved!*

Paul Merson… *Scored!*

Michael… *Scored!*

David Batty… *Saved!*

NOOOOOOOOO, not again! England had been knocked out of a major tournament on penalties for the third time in eight years. First Italia 90, then Euro 96, and now France 98 – surely, they were cursed!

As the Argentina players celebrated, Gareth went over and put his arm around David, just like Stuart had done to him two years before. He tried his best to comfort his teammate and tell him it would all be okay, but he knew from his own experience at Euro 96 that there was nothing he could say to make him feel better.

Two years later, England were back at another major international tournament: Euro 2000, hosted by Belgium and the Netherlands. Kevin Keegan was the new national team manager and Gareth was now the fourth-choice centre-back, behind Tony and Sol, and also Martin Keown.

Oh well, at least he was still in the England squad, and with ten minutes to go in their final group game, Gareth was suddenly called into action. The Three Lions were drawing 2–2 with Romania, a result that would see them finish second in 'The Group of Death', behind Portugal but ahead of Germany, and qualify for the knockout rounds.

Come on, England!

Romania, however, were on the hunt for a winning goal, and so Keegan decided to bring on an extra defender. With Tony already out injured, it was Gareth's job to keep things calm and see his team through to the Last 16.

It was all going according to plan until the eighty-ninth minute, when Viorel Moldovan escaped past Phil Neville and dribbled into the England penalty area. Sol, Martin and Gareth were all there in the middle, ready to deal with the danger, but Phil was determined to get back and make the tackle himself. As he slid in with his left foot, he got his timing all wrong and kicked Moldovan's leg instead of the ball. Penalty!

Noooooooooo!

Ionel Ganea stepped up and… sent Nigel Martyn the wrong way. 3–2 to Romania!

Moments later, the match was over and so was England's Euro 2000 adventure. Afterwards, Gareth wandered around the pitch for ages in shock and disbelief. Had that really just happened? Why did every major tournament seem to end in disaster for England?

CHAPTER 14

MOVING TO... MIDDLESBROUGH!

'If I am to achieve in my career, it is time to move on.'

Days before he left for Euro 2000, Gareth had
handed in a transfer request at Villa. After five years at
the club, he was tired of experiencing the same season
over and over again. Fourth place, fifth, seventh, sixth,
sixth – Villa were always getting close to the top of
the Premier League, but never quite close enough.

To take the next step and really compete with
the big boys like Manchester United, Liverpool,
Arsenal and Newcastle, they needed to have more
ambition and more top-quality players. But as well
as signing new stars, Villa kept selling their old ones.
Mark Bosnich and Dwight were winning trophies

at Manchester United, Savo had been sold to Real Zaragoza, Stan had left to join Leicester City, and Ugo had just moved to Middlesbrough.

At the age of thirty, Gareth was ready for a fresh start too, but where would he go? There was interest from Chelsea, the club who had just beaten them in the FA Cup final and finished one place above them in the Premier League, but there was no way that Villa were going to let him leave for a low fee like £4 million.

'That offer was insulting,' declared the club's chairman, Doug Ellis. 'We know the kind of figure we're looking for and if we don't get it, Gareth will be staying with us.'

£5 million? No, Villa wanted more money for their captain.

£6 million? No, they wanted more than that too.

That turned out to be Chelsea's final bid, so in the end, Gareth had no choice but to stay at Villa for one more season. After that, however, he made his move at last, to…

Middlesbrough!

Really? It was a surprising choice because they weren't one of the big boys of the Premier League. In fact, for the last few seasons, Middlesbrough had finished twelfth and fourteenth, far behind Villa.

The club, however, had much higher ambitions for the future. In recent years, Boro had signed Christian Ziege from AC Milan, Christian Karembeu from Real Madrid, Alen Bokšic from Lazio… and now Gareth from Aston Villa! As well as all the exciting foreign stars, he would also be reunited with some very familiar faces, like Ugo, his England teammate Paul Ince, and one of his old England coaches, Steve McClaren.

McClaren was now the new Middlesbrough manager, and he had a clear vision of what he wanted to do: 'I plan to develop young players at the club and surround them with role models. I want leaders and to fill the team with them.'

A team full of leaders – Gareth fitted that plan perfectly and so in July 2001, he became McClaren's first signing for £6.5 million.

'I really believe that something positive is going to

happen here,' he said as he smiled and held up a red club shirt with 'SOUTHGATE' written on the back in large white letters.

Gareth couldn't wait to play his part in pushing Middlesbrough up the Premier League table. It was great to be back alongside Ugo again, and with the two of them together, the team soon stopped conceding so many goals. Their calm communication and organisation led to cleansheets against West Ham, Blackburn, Everton, their old club Aston Villa, local rivals Sunderland, and best of all, Manchester United.

Away at Old Trafford, Alen gave Middlesbrough an early lead in the ninth minute, and they managed to hold on for the rest of the match, thanks to lots of heroic defending. Beckham, Giggs, and Ruud van Nistelrooy tried and tried, but they couldn't get past Boro's brilliant centre-backs. At the final whistle, they hugged and celebrated a famous victory together in front of the fans.

'Come onnnnnn!' Gareth roared, punching the air three times.

That wonderful win lifted Middlesbrough up to

tenth in the Premier League table, but sadly the
progress didn't last. The problem was that they
weren't scoring enough goals. Alen got eight, but the
next highest was Noel Whelan with just four. In the
last ten league games of the season, the team only
scored seven goals, as they slipped down to twelfth
place again. And after making it through to the FA
Cup semi-finals, they lost 1–0 to Arsenal.

It was a match that summed up Middlesbrough's
frustrating season. Despite creating lots of great
attacking chances, they failed to take any of them,
and then at the other end, Gianluca Festa sliced a
clearance into his own net.

'Why are we so unlucky?!' Gareth groaned as he
trudged off the pitch.

While it hadn't been the glory-filled first season
that he had hoped for, he was still pleased with his
own performances. In forty-four calm, consistent
appearances for Middlesbrough, he had scored one
goal, helped his team to keep seventeen cleansheets,
and most amazingly of all, he hadn't received a single
yellow or red card. For a centre-back, that was an

astonishing record!

Gareth had settled in so smoothly at his new club that at the end of season awards ceremony, he was named Middlesbrough's Player of the Year. And a few months later, when Paul went to Wolves, Gareth was also given the captain's armband.

CHAPTER 15

CAPTAIN
INCREDIBLE

29 February 2004, Millennium Stadium, Cardiff

Eight years after his success with Villa, Gareth had
finally made it back to the League Cup final again.
This time, as Middlesbrough captain, he was standing
right at the front of the line, ready to lead his team out
onto the pitch, and all the way to victory.

In the tunnel, Gareth looked relaxed as he shook
hands with opponents and chatted with the mascots,
but by the time he walked out into the amazing
atmosphere of the Millennium Stadium, his game face
was on. He was fired up and focused on helping his
team to win. If they did, Gareth would become the

first Middlesbrough captain to ever lift a major trophy in the club's 128-year history.

Boro had reached the League Cup final before in 1997 and 1998, plus the FA Cup final in 1997, but on all three occasions, they had finished as runners-up. Could Gareth be the hero who led them to glory at last?

They certainly had the talent to lift the trophy this time. In attack, Middlesbrough had the energy of Gaizka Mendieta, the skill of Bolo Zenden and Juninho, plus the explosive pace of Joseph-Désiré Job. And at the back, they had Gareth and Ugo to keep things calm and organised.

Bolton, however, wouldn't be an easy team to beat. They too had international superstars in their side, like Jay-Jay Okocha, Iván Campo and Youri Djorkaeff. Back in the Premier League, Boro were thirteenth while Bolton were eleventh, so it was all set to be a very even and exciting battle.

As kick-off approached, Gareth walked around high-fiving his teammates and giving them a last pre-match message: 'Let's get straight at them, lads – we want a strong start here!'

The Boro players listened to their leader.

In the first minute, Joseph rushed forward to block Émerson Thome's long ball.

Hurraaaaaaaaay!

Then in the second minute, Gaizka played a beautiful pass to Bolo on the left, who fired a brilliant low cross into the box, where Joseph slid in to score.

Goooooooooooooooooooaaaaaaaaaaaaaaaaaalllllllllllll llllllllllll!!!!!!!!!!!!!!!!!!!!

Middlesbrough were off to a dream start and they didn't stop there. After a one-two with Juninho, Gaizka played the ball forward to Joseph. With a neat flick, he tried to turn past Thome, but the Bolton defender tripped him. *Penalty!*

As he watched from the halfway line, Gareth could hardly believe what he was seeing. It all seemed too good to be true. Bolo slipped as he took the spot-kick, but luckily, the ball still landed safely in the net.

Goooooooooooooooooooaaaaaaaaaaaaaaaaaalllllllllllll llllllllllll!!!!!!!!!!!!!!!!!!!!

A lead of 2–0 after just seven minutes! Boro would

never get a better chance to win a trophy, but Gareth knew that it wasn't game over yet. Once Bolton recovered from the shock, they would have some defending to do...

BLOCK! Gareth stretched out his long left leg to stop Nicky Hunt's cross from entering the six-yard box.

HEADER! He leapt up and won the ball against Bolton's strong striker, Kevin Davies.

CLEARANCE! He calmly chested the ball down and booted it away before Kevin Nolan could reach it.

In the twentieth minute, Gareth chased back to close Davies down as he ran towards the Boro box. The angle was tight and his shot wasn't particularly powerful, but somehow it slipped through Mark Schwarzer's gloves and into the net. *2–1!*

Nooooooooooooooo!

Suddenly, Bolton were back in the game, and Boro needed their captain's influence more than ever. But Gareth didn't get angry and start yelling; no, that wasn't his style at all. To win the League Cup final, they were all going to need to keep calm and work together as a team. So instead, he used his voice to organise his players, give them advice, and praise them when they did something good.

'Hey, slow it down!' he called out when Bolo tried to take a quick free kick.

'Well done!' he clapped when Franck Queudrue headed the ball back to his keeper.

'Well held!' he cheered when Mark saved a shot from Okocha.

Middlesbrough were still winning 2–1 at half-time, and they were still winning 2–1 with ten minutes to go. The trophy was in sight, but Gareth made sure that his teammates stayed switched on until the very end.

Mark punched away Bruno Ngotty's long ball forward.

'Yessssss, Schwarz!'

Ugo threw himself bravely in front of Stelios Giannakopoulos to block his shot.

'That's it – keep going!' Gareth shouted, giving his partner a pat on the back.

Stelios dribbled into the box at speed, but Franck

was there to stop him.

'Almost there now, lads – one last push!'

Second by second, the time ticked away until the final whistle blew. They had done it; they had made history. Middlesbrough had won a major trophy for the first time ever!

What a moment, what a feeling, and what an achievement! While the fans went wild up in the stands, their heroes celebrated in different ways down on the pitch. Juninho was clapping, Franck was crying, and Gareth? At first, he walked around hugging and high-fiving all the Middlesbrough players and coaches, looking as calm as ever. The only change was the big, beaming smile on his face.

Once the TV interviews were over, however, Gareth finally let his captain's composure slip. He ran towards the fans with the armband in his hand and punched the air once, twice, and then a third time.

'Come onnnnnnnnn!' he roared with pride and passion, and the supporters roared right back. Gareth had been a club hero already, but now after leading the team to glory, he was an absolute legend.

Eventually, it was time for the moment everyone was waiting for: the new greatest moment in the history of Middlesbrough Football Club. With the lights out and his teammates all behind him, Gareth stepped forward to collect the cup.

'Right, ready?' he checked over his shoulder.

Yesssssssssssssssssssssssssss!

Ooooooohhhhhhhhhhhhhh…

After a short dramatic pause, Gareth kissed the trophy and raised it high above his head.

…Hurrrraaaaaaaaaaaaaaayyyyy!

Then as fireworks filled the Cardiff sky, Boro's Captain Incredible bounced up and down with delight. It was a day that would live with Gareth forever.

CHAPTER 16

A FINAL
FAREWELL

10 May 2006, Philips Stadion, Eindhoven

After sixteen years, the time had come for Gareth to play his final game as a professional footballer. Rather than let his form and fitness fade away slowly, however, he had decided to go out on the highest of highs, by captaining his club in the 2006 UEFA Cup final.

Yes, just two years on from lifting the League Cup, Gareth's Middlesbrough team were close to an even greater achievement. In their second-ever season in Europe, they had made it all the way, past:

VfB Stuttgart of Germany,

AS Roma of Italy,

FC Basel of Switzerland,

And Steaua Bucharest of Romania.

Now, they were just one game away from lifting the UEFA Cup trophy! That one huge game, however, was against a very strong Sevilla side, featuring Brazilians Dani Alves and Luís Fabiano, as well as Argentinian striker Javier Saviola.

Middlesbrough didn't mind being the underdogs, though. Anything could happen in a single game of football, and as they had already shown many times in the tournament, they had great goalscorers of their own. For the final, they had Jimmy Floyd Hasselbaink and Mark Viduka up front, with Yakubu Aiyegbeni and Massimo Maccarone both waiting impatiently on the bench.

Boro! Boro! Boro!

As he led his team out onto the pitch for the last time, Gareth was so focused that he hardly noticed the giant UEFA Cup trophy in front of him. Yes, Middlesbrough had done so well to get to the final, but they weren't there just to take part. They were there to try and win a second major trophy.

Boro! Boro! Boro!

A lot of the team had changed since the League Cup win in 2004. Bolo, Juninho and Joseph had left the club, Gaizka was injured, and Ugo was on the bench, but they still had Mark Schwarzer in goal, George Boateng in midfield, and most importantly, their captain Gareth keeping things calm and classy at the back.

'Let's get straight at them, lads,' he clapped and cheered one last time. 'We want a strong start here!'

Sadly, however, there were no early goals for Boro this time. They survived the first twenty-five minutes, but soon after that, Sevilla took the lead. As Dani Alves got the ball on the right, Gareth was marking Saviola and his new centre-back partner, Chris Riggott, was supposed to be marking Luís Fabiano. When the cross came in, however, the Brazilian somehow had a free header and he took full advantage. *1–0!*

Noooooooooooo!

Gareth did his best to hide his frustration, but he knew from experience how crucial the first goal in a final could be. It was far from over yet, though. Middlesbrough had fought back from 3–0 down to win their semi-final against Steaua Bucharest, so why couldn't they do it again? Mark Viduka's powerful strike was saved, Massimo came on and almost caught out the Sevilla keeper, and then Jimmy curled a free kick just over the bar.

'Unlucky – keep going!' McClaren shouted encouragement from the sidelines.

Middlesbrough pushed further and further forward, searching for an equaliser, until eventually, Sevilla punished them on the counter-attack. Mark Schwarzer managed to stop Fréddie Kanouté's shot, but the rebound fell straight to Enzo Maresca. *2–0!*

From down on the grass, Gareth looked up to see the ball land in the net and then let his head and shoulders drop. Surely it was game over now? Just to make sure, Sevilla scored two more goals in the last ten minutes to add to Middlesbrough's misery.

For Gareth, there would be no fairytale ending to his story as a footballer, but as he walked slowly around the pitch afterwards shaking hands, he felt proud as well as disappointed. He was proud of his teammates, who had exceeded all expectations by taking Middlesbrough to their first-ever European final. It was an amazing experience that none of the players or fans would ever forget.

And Gareth was proud of himself too as he looked back on his long and eventful career. As a youngster, he had been rejected by Southampton and then relegated twice with Crystal Palace, but look at him now! Thanks to years of hard work and resilience, he was retiring after captaining his club in the UEFA Cup final, lifting two League Cup trophies, and winning fifty-seven caps for his country.

The kid from Crawley had grown up to achieve his England dream and so much more, but he wasn't saying goodbye to the game he loved. No, no, Gareth was soon moving straight on to his next great challenge, as Middlesbrough's new manager.

CHAPTER 17

MIDDLESBROUGH'S NEW MANAGER

The news had broken a week before the UEFA Cup final: McClaren was about to become the new England manager. Gareth was delighted for his boss, but what did that mean for Middlesbrough? Who would their next manager be?

Former Celtic and Leicester boss Martin O'Neill was the favourite to get the job, but the Boro chairman, Steve Gibson, decided to go for a different option. After talking to Terry Venables, Gibson gave Gareth a call and asked him a question that really caught him by surprise:

'How would you feel about becoming the new Middlesbrough manager?'

What?! At first, he was too shocked to reply. Surely, it was too soon for that? He was still only thirty-six, and he didn't feel ready for the responsibility of running a Premier League club. Besides, he hadn't even got the right coaching qualifications yet!

The idea of Gareth becoming a football manager wasn't a surprise to any of the players and coaches who had worked with him before, though.

Communication? *Tick!*

Organisation? *Tick!*

Leadership? *Tick!*

Calm under pressure? *Tick!*

A fantastic football brain? *Tick!*

Everyone knew that he had all the skills he would need to succeed.

After some time to think, Gareth realised that it was an amazing opportunity that he had to take. Yes, he was being thrown in at the deep end with no experience, but he loved a challenge. So, he signed a five-year contract as Middlesbrough's new manager and got straight to work on completing his coaching qualifications.

At first, Gareth found his new job very, very stressful. With the 2006–07 Premier League season approaching fast, there was so much for him to think about. What formation would he use for his Middlesbrough team, and what style of football would they play? Which new players should they sign, and who should they sell? Plus, how would his friends and former teammates feel about him being their boss now?

Gareth didn't really know any of the answers. It was all so new to him, so he asked Malcolm Crosby, one of Middlesbrough's most experienced coaches, to be his assistant, and together they worked hard to prepare as much as possible for the season ahead.

Boro signed:

Robert Huth to replace Gareth at centre-back, as well as Jonathan Woodgate on loan from Real Madrid,

Julio Arca from local rivals Sunderland to be their new left-back,

And Jason Euell as an extra option in attack.

For their opening game away at Reading, Gareth decided to go with his favourite formation from his days at Villa: 3–5–2. The aim was to stay solid at the back and use the pace and power of Mark Viduka and Yakubu on the attack. For the first forty minutes, the plan seemed to work perfectly. Stewart Downing volleyed in the first goal and Yakubu tapped in the second. *2–0!*

What a start! Maybe being a manager wasn't so hard after all… But just as Gareth was planning a happy half-time team-talk, everything changed. In the space of two minutes, they conceded two sloppy goals. *2–2!* Then early in the second half, the Middlesbrough defence messed up again and allowed Leroy Lita to score the winner.

For Gareth, it was a harsh welcome to life as a football manager, but he was determined to keep going, and so were his players. Four days later, Boro bounced back to beat Chelsea 2–1, thanks to a last-minute winner from Mark Viduka. *Phew!*

It turned out to be a season full of ups and downs for Middlesbrough, but in charge of each game, Gareth grew more comfortable and more confident in his new role. Although he was still learning all the time, he didn't feel like the nervous new kid anymore.

With a 3–1 win over Fulham, Middlesbrough finished twelfth, two places higher than the previous year. It wasn't a huge improvement, but there were certainly reasons to feel positive. Gareth believed in giving young academy players a chance, and they were starting to shine: Stewart, Lee Cattermole and James Morrison in midfield, plus Andrew Taylor, Matthew Bates and David Wheater in defence. They were the future of the football club, and that's why Gareth had made the difficult decision to let older players like Ray Parlour and his good friend, Ugo, leave.

New season, new challenge – could Middlesbrough push on up the Premier League table? Sadly, Yakubu had signed for Everton and Viduka for Newcastle, so Gareth had the tough task of building a brand-new strikeforce. During the summer, he signed Jérémie Aliadière from Arsenal, Mido from Tottenham, and Tuncay from Turkish club Fenerbahçe, but by Christmas, they had only scored five goals between them, and Boro were only three points above the relegation zone.

What should Gareth do? In the January transfer

window, he decided to take a risk and buy a new striker for a club-record fee of £12 million. Afonso Alves had scored goal after goal for Dutch team Heerenveen, but could he do it in the Premier League? That was the big question.

Although the Brazilian wasn't a huge success, he did help Middlesbrough to turn their season around by scoring five goals in two unforgettable matches against the Manchester clubs. First, Afonso scored both goals in a 2–2 draw with United, and then, on the final day, he scored a hat-trick in a record win over City. What a way to end the season – an 8–1 win!

'Bring on next year!' the Boro supporters thought as they left the Riverside Stadium that afternoon, and their excitement grew as the team started the new campaign well, beating Tottenham and Stoke City. Gareth even won the Premier League Manager of the Month award for August.

After that, however, it all fell apart for Middlesbrough. Afonso and the other strikers stopped scoring, and from mid-November through to February, they played fourteen league games without winning a single one. Uh-oh – they were in big relegation trouble now. Gareth tried everything to solve the problem – different players, different tactics, different formations – but nothing seemed to work. Eventually, the bad run ended against Liverpool, but the next week, Boro went straight back to losing again.

Booooooooooooooooooooooooooooo!

You don't know what you're doing!

We want Southgate sacked!

As a player, Gareth had been a club hero, but now that he was the manager and the team was struggling, the fans had turned against him. Apparently, it was all his fault.

'Come on, keep going – we can still stay up!'

Gareth did his best to lift the players, but with each bad result, their confidence levels dropped lower and lower. On the last day of the season, Boro needed a miracle to survive, and sadly it didn't arrive. After eleven years in the Premier League, they were going down.

Gareth was devastated but he refused to give up. 'It's a low for our football club, our supporters, our players and our staff,' he said. 'It's a painful blow but we have to take the pain and move forward.'

As a captain, he had led Crystal Palace back to the Premier League, and now he planned to do the same as a manager with Middlesbrough.

It wasn't going to be easy in a difficult division like the Championship, but with thirteen games played, Boro were right on track for promotion. They sat fourth in the table, just one point off top spot, so Gareth wasn't too worried when he got a call asking him to go the chairman's office. As soon as he entered the room, however, he could tell that something bad was about to happen.

'I'm sorry, Gareth, this is the hardest decision I've ever had to make,' Gibson told him, 'but it's time for us to make a change.'

Just like that, after three-and-a-half seasons, Gareth's time as Middlesbrough manager was over. He couldn't believe it – an hour earlier, his team had beaten Derby 2–0, so why was he being sacked now? It didn't make any sense.

As the news spread fast around the football world,

Gareth felt so hurt and humiliated, but he had been through worse before. Having experienced the pain of missing a crucial penalty for England, he knew that he could bounce back from anything.

Gareth decided to take some time away from the game to rest and recover. And then? He didn't know yet, but despite the disappointing end, his first taste of being a football manager had definitely left him wanting more.

CHAPTER 18

WORKING WITH ENGLAND'S RISING STARS

After going straight from a long playing career to Middlesbrough manager, it felt good for Gareth to step away from the game for a while. For the next few years, he enjoyed doing all of the things that he hadn't had time to do before. He spent lots of time with his family, ran his first marathon, and talked about football on TV.

Eventually, however, Gareth was offered an exciting new opportunity, and in January 2011, he accepted the role as the FA's Head of Elite Development. It was a fancy title, but essentially, his job was to try and improve the standard of youth football across the country, and so help England to produce better players for the future.

Gareth was really glad to be back in football and he found that he loved his new job, especially the hours spent working with England's rising stars. There were so many talented young players around, but the challenge was helping them to make the most of their potential. How could they create the best possible pathway for them to follow, from the England youth teams through to the senior team? And how could coaches develop more technical footballers like in France, Spain and Germany? Finding the answers to these questions quickly became Gareth's new passion.

Two years later, another exciting new opportunity arrived. Gareth's old international teammate Stuart Pearce had been the manager of the England Under-21s since 2007, but after six years in the job, the FA had decided that it was time for a change. Would Gareth be interested in taking over?

Yes, he would! By then, it was four years since he'd left Middlesbrough, and Gareth finally felt ready to go back and give management another go. Plus, as the coach of the England Under-21s, he would be able

to carry on his youth development work at the same
time.

'I'm extremely excited about the prospect of
working with the best and brightest young players
in the country,' Gareth said after signing a three-year
contract.

The Under-21s had lost all three of their games
at the recent 2013 European Championships, so
Gareth decided that it was time for a fresh start.
He had a clear vision of the new England he was
aiming to build: skilful on the ball, but also strong
both physically and mentally. And he also now had a
clear vision of the kind of manager he wanted to be.
Although his time at Middlesbrough had ended badly,
Gareth had learned a lot from the experience. Of
course, he wanted his team to win football matches,
but he also wanted to get to know his players and help
them to improve through talking rather than shouting.

For his first match in charge against Moldova,
Gareth made six changes, bringing in:

John Stones, Michael Keane and Luke Shaw in
defence,

James Ward-Prowse and Tom Carroll in midfield,
And Saido Berahino in attack.

Gareth's new England got off to the perfect start as
three of the new players combined for the opening
goal. From the right, Stones moved the ball infield to
Carroll, who slid a clever pass through to Saido, who
fired a shot into the top corner. *1–0!*

On the sidelines, Gareth clapped and smiled. It
was exactly the sort of smart, passing football that he
wanted his Under-21s to play. Although they failed
to score a second goal, they dominated the game and
the defence hardly had any work to do. At the final
whistle, Gareth celebrated his first win in charge and
there were lots more wins to come as the goals began
to flow:

San Marino 0 England 4,
England 5 Lithuania 0,
England 3 Finland 0,
England 9 San Marino 0!

With thirty-five goals scored and only four
conceded, Gareth's team qualified for the 2015
European Championships without losing a single

match. There would be tougher tests ahead, though, and so to prepare for the tournament, the England Under-21s played friendlies against two of the top European teams: Portugal and France.

Portugal's line-up featured Bruno Fernandes, Bernardo Silva, Rúben Neves and Ricardo Pereira, but Gareth's new England beat them 3–1, thanks to two goals from Danny Ings. Now, could they travel to France and win there too? Harry Kane scored twice to give England the lead, but *Les Bleus* fought back brilliantly with Kingsley Coman scoring the winner.

Oh no, in his fourteenth game in charge, Gareth's Under-21s had finally been beaten, but when he walked back into the dressing room after the match, he didn't get angry or frustrated. Instead, he focused on the positives and the lessons that his players could learn from the experience.

'We'll need to defend a lot better if we're going to win the Euros next summer,' he told his team calmly. 'We can't throw away 2–0 leads like that.'

England had been drawn in a really difficult group with Portugal, Sweden and Italy. Every game was going to be a serious challenge, so which players would Gareth select in his starting line-up?

With Saido out injured, he picked a front three of Nathan Redmond, Jesse Lingard and Harry Kane for their opening match against Portugal, but for the first time, Gareth's Young Lions failed to score a single goal. Portugal, however, did, with João Mário tapping in the winner. *1–0!*

Oh dear, it was a disastrous start for England, but their calm manager didn't panic. The team would just have to beat Sweden now. At half-time, however, it was still 0–0, so Gareth made some attacking substitutions and eventually, the goal arrived. In the eighty-fifth minute, Jesse chested the ball down and smashed a powerful shot past the keeper. *1–0!*

Phew, England's Euro dream was still alive! Now, if they could avoid defeat in their last group game against Italy, they would be through to the semi-finals. That didn't sound too difficult, but the Young Lions switched off, conceding two goals in two minutes in the first half. Although they tried to turn things around in the second, it was too little too late.

England were heading home.

Despite his disappointment, Gareth refused to give up, or to name, blame and shame. His Young Lions won together, they lost together, and they learned together. 'These are young players and there's some improvement that needs to happen in terms of their general defending as a group and as individuals,' was all he said to the media afterwards. Then, Gareth moved straight on to preparing his players for their next challenge: the 2016 Toulon Tournament.

France were the hosts and they had invited nine other top teams from all over the world: Paraguay, Mexico, Japan, Guinea, Mali, Portugal, Bulgaria, the Czech Republic and England. By then, players like Harry, Jesse, Luke and John had moved up to the senior team, so it was a great chance for Gareth to give some new Young Lions a shot at glory.

Lewis Baker scored the goals as they won 1–0 against Portugal and Japan;

Jack Grealish and Cauley Woodrow grabbed two goals each as England thrashed Guinea 7–1…

…And Ruben Loftus-Cheek was the hero as they

hammered Paraguay 4–0.

With four wins out of four, England were through to the final of the Toulon Tournament, where they faced… France.

James played a brilliant long ball to Lewis, who headed it into the net. *1–0!*

Nathan threaded a pass through to Ruben, who lifted it over the rushing keeper. *2–0!*

The Young Lions had a 2–0 lead against France again, but this time, they didn't lose it. At the final whistle, the tired players threw their arms in the air. England had won the Toulon Tournament for the first time since 1994!

Gareth was delighted to win his first trophy as a manager, but the moment wasn't about him; it was about his amazing group of players. So, he stood to the side and smiled as they bounced up and down together.

Campeones, Campeones, Olé! Olé! Olé!

Next up for the England Under-21s: the 2017 Euros in Poland. By then, however, their manager had moved on to take an even bigger job.

CHAPTER 19

FROM ENGLAND JUNIORS TO SENIORS

Gareth was first offered the senior England job in June 2016, just days after the team's embarrassing defeat to Iceland at the Euros, and just weeks after his own Under-21 team had won the Toulon Tournament. After thinking about it, Gareth decided to say no for two reasons:

1) He was really enjoying his work with the England juniors,

And

2) He didn't think he was ready for such a high-pressure role yet. What if he failed again like he had at Middlesbrough? Managing England was famously one of the toughest tasks in football.

In July, Sam Allardyce was named as the new man in charge instead, but by September, England were already looking for another new manager...

Gareth? This time, when the FA asked him, he agreed to become the caretaker manager, at least for the next few matches anyway. As he had shown as a player, when his country really needed him, he was always ready to step forward and take responsibility.

For his first game against Malta, Gareth stuck with six of the England team which had lost to Iceland: Joe Hart in goal, Kyle Walker and Gary Cahill in defence, Dele Alli and Wayne Rooney in midfield, and Daniel Sturridge up front. To that experienced core, he then added four exciting young players who he already knew well from the Under-21s:

Left-back Danny Rose,

Centre-back John Stones,

Defensive midfielder Jordan Henderson,

And attacking midfielder Jesse Lingard.

The result was a comfortable 2–0 victory, with goals from Daniel and Dele.

Just like with the England Under-21s, Gareth was

off to a winning start. Could he keep it up?

Slovenia 0 England 0,

England 3 Scotland 0,

England 2 Spain 2

Two wins, two draws and zero defeats – it was enough to earn Gareth the job on a permanent basis, and this time he accepted.

'I am extremely proud to be appointed England manager,' he told the journalists. 'Now I want to do the job successfully.'

Now that he was no longer the caretaker, Gareth was determined to do things his own way: his players, his tactics, his style of football. His vision was the same as it had been for the England juniors: to build a team that was skilful on the ball, but also strong both physically and mentally. A team that was capable of winning major international tournaments.

In order to achieve that goal, Gareth believed that England needed to look to the future, even if that meant making some tough decisions. So, over the next few months, out went older players like Rooney, Sturridge, Adam Lallana, and Jamie Vardy, and in came fresher young talents like Raheem Sterling, Harry Kane, Alex Oxlade-Chamberlain, and Marcus Rashford. It was a risky move, but it worked out really well. England finished top of their qualification group for the 2018 World Cup without losing a single game.

'Russia, here we come!' the players and supporters celebrated together at Wembley.

Gareth had successfully guided England to the world's greatest football tournament, but did he stop to relax and enjoy the moment? Oh no, he decided that it was the right time to make even more changes:

Goalkeeper Joe Hart out, Jordan Pickford in,

Centre-back Gary Cahill out, Harry Maguire in,

Right-back Nathaniel Clyne out, Kieran Trippier in,

And most significant of all,

4–3–3 out, 3–5–2 in!

Yes, Gareth turned to his favourite formation from his playing days: a back three with wing-backs. The idea was that an extra defender would make England much harder to beat at the World Cup, but would it work? In the months leading up to the tournament, Gareth tested it out against four top teams:

Germany – 0–0,

Brazil – 0–0,

Netherlands – 1–0 to England,

Italy – 1–1.

Hurray, their new formation certainly seemed to be working; they were now very hard to beat!

In May 2018, when Gareth announced his final twenty-three-man World Cup squad, it was one of the youngest England groups ever, and one of the most varied too. Whereas previous teams had been centred around Liverpool, Chelsea and Manchester United players, Gareth's chosen twenty-three came from lots of different clubs, including Leicester City, Tottenham, Stoke City and Everton, and many of them had shown the strength and resilience to rise up from the lower leagues. Now, they were all on the same team, working together towards the same goal: winning the World Cup for England.

'We think this is the best group of players available,' Gareth told the media confidently. 'We think they can be very exciting now and even more exciting in the future.'

With the Premier League season over, Gareth set to work, getting his exciting England stars properly prepared for the World Cup. As he knew from his own painful experiences as a player and a manager, major tournament football was just as much about team spirit and mindset, as it was about talent. So, on top of the normal training sessions for fitness and tactics, Gareth also organised:

1) a surprise trip with the Royal Marines, where the players had to spend the night living in woods and searching for their own food, before completing a tough endurance course together. Although some of them definitely didn't enjoy it at the time, it really helped to form a strong bond between everyone.

2) a lot of penalty practice! But Gareth didn't just get his players to keep shooting from the spot; to recreate the real thing, he also got them to do the long walk from the halfway line and at the end of training sessions when they were really tired.

3) a top sports psychologist to travel to Russia with the squad. Gareth didn't want his young England players to feel weighed down by the pressure from the

fans or the failures of the past. They were a brand-new team and to perform at their best, they needed to feel fresh, focused and fearless out on the pitch.

When the players arrived at the team hotel in Russia, they each found personalised, handwritten notes from Gareth in their rooms. The overall message was the same for everyone, though:

'Be brave and go for it!'

Right, Gareth and his coaches had done everything possible to prepare the England players for the tournament. Now, it was time for the World Cup to kick off.

CHAPTER 20

WORLD CUP 2018: A BRAVE NEW ENGLAND ERA

England got off to a great start in their opening World Cup match against Tunisia. In the tenth minute, Ashley Young swung a corner into the box, and up jumped John to meet it with a powerful header. The goalkeeper made a good save, but the rebound dropped to their new captain and star striker, Harry Kane, who reacted in a flash. *1–0!*

Hurraaaaaaaaay!

As the England players piled on top of Harry in front of the fans, Gareth stood on the sidelines in his smart suit and waistcoat and allowed a small smile to spread across his face. Yes, things were going well so far, but he wasn't getting carried away just yet. This was tournament football, where anything could happen...

Just when the Three Lions were looking comfortable in the game, Kyle Walker challenged for the ball in his own box and the referee awarded a penalty to Tunisia.

'No way!' the England players complained furiously, but it was no use arguing. The decision had been made and up stepped Ferjani Sassi to equalise. 1–1 – game on!

When the match restarted, Gareth urged his team to stay calm and stick to the plan. There was no need to panic; England still had plenty of time left to score a winning goal.

When the goal hadn't arrived after sixty-five minutes, however, Gareth decided to make his first substitution: Raheem Sterling off, and Marcus on. That gave England a bit more energy in attack, but still the goal wouldn't come. As the minutes ticked by, the fans grew restless and the players got more and more frustrated. A draw wasn't good enough; they needed to win!

'Keep going, guys!' Gareth called out

encouragement. 'It's not over yet – we've just got to be patient.'

It was a real test of his team's togetherness and mindset – could they somehow find a way to score?

In the ninetieth minute, Kieran curled one last corner into the box. This time, it was Harry Maguire who jumped the highest, flicking the ball on to Harry Kane, who stayed calm and steered his header past the keeper. *2–1 to England!*

HURRAAAAAAAAAY!

Gareth leapt up out of his seat and punched the air with joy and relief. What an important goal, what an important win!

Thankfully, England's next victory, against Panama, was a lot less stressful.

Kieran crossed and John headed home. *1–0!*

Harry smashed in an unstoppable penalty. *2–0!*

Jesse curled a long-range shot into the top corner. *3–0!*

John finished off a brilliant team move. *4–0!*

Harry scored from the spot again. *5–0!*

Ruben Loftus-Cheek's fluke shot flicked up off

Harry's heel to complete his hat-trick. *6–0!*

'H, that's the worst hat-trick ever!' Jesse Lingard joked afterwards.

So far, the World Cup was going even better than Gareth had expected. England were through to the knockout rounds already, and the team spirit was at an all-time high. The players were getting on really well and enjoying themselves, both on and off the pitch. At their base camp in Repino, Gareth had organised for the team to have a ten-pin bowling alley, a snooker table, air hockey and table football tables, and a dartboard to keep everyone entertained and, of course, competitive.

'Come on, I bet you can't beat me!' the players challenged each other.

And that wasn't all. With only a few days between each match, Gareth wanted to make the most of the recovery time. So he sent his squad off to the swimming pool and threw in some inflatable unicorns for them to race around on!

'Have fun! Just don't hurt each other, okay?'

'Thanks boss – you're the best!'

After escaping from the World Cup pressure for a while, the players felt fresh and ready for their Round of 16 clash with Colombia. It wasn't going to be easy to beat a team with top players like Yerry Mina, Juan Cuadrado and Falcao, but Gareth's new England had the nation behind them again. After years of failure and disappointment, the hope and excitement were back:

'It's coming home, it's coming home,
It's coming, FOOTBALL'S COMING HOME!'

That was the aim, and when Harry Kane gave England the lead early in the second half, it looked like they were on their way to the World Cup quarter-finals. With seconds to go, however, Colombia scored an equaliser.

Noooooooooooooo! What now?

'We go again,' Gareth told his tired players during the break before extra-time. It was another huge test of his team's togetherness and mindset. Could they remain united and resilient? Yes, but after making it

through thirty more minutes, the game went to…
PENALTIES!

Uh-oh – that word struck fear in every England fan.
But after failing in 1990, 1998, and 2006, could they
finally win their first-ever World Cup shoot-out?

Gareth and his coaches had prepared the team so
well for this moment. They had practised the long
walk from the halfway line when they were feeling
exhausted, and their keeper, Jordan, had notes about
all the Colombian players written on his drink bottle.

'Come on, we can do this!' Gareth urged them on.

Harry scored, and so did Marcus, but then Jordan
Henderson's spot-kick was saved.

Noooooooooooooo, not again!

But Gareth's England team didn't give up; they
bounced back and turned things around.

First, Mateus Uribe hit the crossbar,

Then Kieran stayed calm and scored,

Then Jordan made a super save to keep out Carlos
Bacca's strike.

Advantage England! On the sideline, Gareth
showed no emotion, but Eric Dier now just needed to

keep cool and...

Gooooooooooooooooooaaaaaaaaaaaaaaaalllllllllllllll llllllllllll!!!!!!!!!!!!!!!!!!!!

What a moment – England were through to
the World Cup quarter-finals after WINNING ON
PENALTIES!

HURRAAAAAAAAAY!

Gareth pumped his fists with pride and hugged his
team of coaches. All their preparation had paid off!
Twenty-two years on from his own painful experience
at Euro 96, it was like a weight had been lifted off his
shoulders. But after a short celebration, Gareth went
over to comfort the two Colombians who had missed
because he knew how they felt.

That was the type of person he was, and the type
of manager too – kind and caring. From the very
beginning, Gareth had known that he wouldn't get
the best out of his England team by shouting and
swearing. No, he believed in talking to his players
calmly and honestly about ways they could improve,
and that approach was working because they were
through to the World Cup quarter-finals!

Sweden were England's next opponents, and
thankfully, there was no penalty drama this time.
Instead, Gareth's side put on their best performance
yet. The first goal was another England set-piece
special. Ashley's corner was brilliant, and Harry
Maguire's header was even better. *1–0!*

Then, early in the second half, England's attacking
midfielders teamed up to secure the win. Jesse
chipped a high ball towards the back post, where Dele
was waiting to head it in. *2–0!*

England were through to the World Cup semi-finals
for the first time since 1990, and they were making
it look easy! The way they were playing together as a
team, they believed they could beat anyone, including
Luka Modric's Croatia. In the fifth minute of the
match, Kieran stepped up and curled a fantastic free
kick into the top corner. *1–0!*

'It's coming home, it's coming home,
It's coming, FOOTBALL'S COMING HOME!'

The England players and fans went absolutely wild,

but their manager stayed as calm as ever. It was far too early to start daydreaming about the World Cup final, when there were still eighty-five minutes of the semi-final to go.

'Come on, keep your concentration!'

Harry Kane almost scored a second for England before half-time, but in the second half, Croatia began to win the midfield battle. Although Jesse and Dele were doing their best to track back and help out Jordan Henderson, they were no match for Modric, Ivan Rakitic and Marcelo Brozovic in the middle. England had problems out wide too, where the Croatia full-backs were pushing forward and finding lots of space.

As his team dropped deeper and deeper, Gareth tried to work out what to do. Something had to change, but what – one player or the whole system? Should he swap Dele or Jesse for another box-to-box midfielder like Ruben, or bring on someone more defensive like Eric or Fabian Delph, or even switch from a back three to a back four?

But by the time he'd made up his mind, it was too

late. Šime Vrsaljko delivered a dangerous cross from the right and Ivan Perišic beat Kyle to the ball. *1–1!*

Noooooooooooooo! What now? In the end, Gareth decided to leave both Dele and Jesse on the pitch, despite their tired legs, and make just one straight swap: Marcus for Raheem up front.

England battled on into extra-time, but there would be no penalty shoot-out this time. In the 110th minute, Mario Mandžukic fired home to win it for Croatia.

NOOOOOOOOOOOOOOO! At the final whistle, England's heroes collapsed on the grass, exhausted and heartbroken. Their World Cup dream was over.

After congratulating the Croatia manager, Gareth walked around the pitch, trying to comfort his players.

'Don't worry, we'll be back,' he assured Harry Kane, putting an arm around his shoulder, 'and we'll be even stronger after tonight.'

They had given absolutely everything for their country and he was so proud of every single one of them. Although they hadn't brought the World Cup home, they had brought football home. Thanks to their fearless performances, England had fallen in love with its national team again. Thousands of fans stayed behind in the stadium to clap and cheer for their heroes, and Gareth led his team over to thank them for their amazing support.

Hopefully, this was just the beginning of a brave new England era. Euro 2020 was only two years away, and before that, they had a brand-new European tournament to try and win.

CHAPTER 21

A NEW FORMATION IN THE NATIONS LEAGUE

Although reaching the 2018 World Cup semi-finals was a great achievement, Gareth believed that his England team were capable of doing even better.

'This is a good moment to build on what we've done, that's how we should view it,' he announced afterwards.

Yes, Colombia and Sweden were both good teams to beat, but in order to take the next step and win a major tournament, they needed more experience against the world's best international teams. With that in mind, the new UEFA Nations League looked like an excellent test for England. As one of the top seeds, they were in a group with Spain and... Croatia. Ooooooh – a chance for revenge!

For the first game against Spain, Gareth stuck with his 3–5–2 World Cup formation and most of his World Cup players too. There were only three changes to the starting line-up:

In the back three – Kyle out, and Joe Gomez in,

At left wing-back – Ashley out, and Luke Shaw in,

And up front – Raheem out, and Marcus in.

It turned out to be a case of same old formation, same old story. Once again, England took an early lead. Luke played a brilliant ball through to Marcus, who scored with a first-time finish. *1–0!*

And once again, they gave it away and lost the game:

Rodrigo crossed to Saúl Ñíguez. *1–1!*

Then Rodrigo flicked on Thiago's free kick. *2–1 to Spain!*

England were unlucky to have a last-minute equaliser disallowed, but still, the match ended in another defeat and it was Gareth's first defeat at home at Wembley. After discussing things with his coaches, he decided that it was time to make more changes.

Against both Croatia and Spain, England's main problem had been their midfield. With Jordan Henderson sitting deep and Jesse and Dele pushing forward to join the attack, the team was struggling to keep the ball and struggling to win it back too. The shape and balance felt wrong. So, a month later, for the first rematch with Croatia, Gareth picked five different players, and most importantly, he lined them up in a different formation: a 4–3–3.

The downside was that England would now have one less defender, but the big upside was that they would have one extra forward, and more space for passers rather than runners in midfield. If they could keep the ball better, they would create more chances, and score more goals – that was Gareth's clever plan.

England's first game with their new formation ended in a 0–0 draw, but in their next Nations League match away in Spain, the new front three was on fire, especially in the first half.

Marcus slid a great pass through to Raheem. *1–0!*

Harry Kane spun beautifully and set up Marcus. *2–0!*

Harry Kane clipped the ball across Raheem. *3–0!*

'This is more like it!' Gareth smiled to himself as he watched from the sidelines. The new system suited

Raheem much better because he preferred playing on the wing and using his speed to cut inside and score.

Spain pulled two goals back in the second half, but England held on for a huge victory over one of the world's best international teams. Now, could they do it again, versus Croatia at Wembley? Not only was it a chance for World Cup revenge, but if they won, they would also go through to the UEFA Nations League Finals.

'Come on, we can do this!' Gareth urged his players on.

This time, it was Croatia who scored first, and England who fought back, with the home fans cheering them on.

Jesse was there in the right place to tap the ball into an empty net. *1–1!*

Then with five minutes to go, Harry Kane slid in to score the winner. *2–1!*

'Yesssssssssssss!' Gareth yelled, throwing both arms up and then punching the air with passion. His resilient young team refused to be beaten. Now, they were off to Portugal, and only two games away from potentially winning a trophy!

First up, in the semi-finals, England faced the Netherlands. Sadly, Harry Kane wasn't fit enough to start the match, so Gareth had to rearrange his front three. Marcus moved into the middle and Raheem switched wings to the left to make space for new young star Jadon Sancho on the right.

After a slow and sloppy start, England took the lead in the thirtieth minute. Marcus reacted quickly to a slip from Matthijs de Ligt and reached the ball just before the defender, who kicked him in the shin. Marcus picked himself up and slotted home the penalty. *1–0!*

'Right, now keep your concentration!' Gareth called out to his players.

What England really needed was a second goal to settle the nerves, but Jadon and John both missed good chances. Then, in the seventy-third minute, de Ligt made up for his earlier mistake by heading home the equaliser. *1–1!*

Noooooooooooooooo, not again! Gareth couldn't believe it – another big game, another lead thrown away. But the England players didn't let their heads drop. With ten minutes to go, Jesse thought he'd scored the winner, but VAR ruled it out for offside. Instead, the game went to extra-time, which turned out to be a step too far for the tired England players.

At the back, John took too long on the ball and gave it away to Memphis Depay. His shot was saved by Jordan, but the rebound deflected in off Kyle. *2–1!*

Ross Barkley got his pass all wrong and played it straight to Depay, who set up Quincy Promes. *3–1!*

The Netherlands, not England, were going through to the Nations League Final. It was so disappointing to lose in another semi-final, and especially like that, after coming so close to victory and then making such silly mistakes. The only positives Gareth could find were that at least it was another learning experience for his young England players, and their tournament wasn't over yet. There was still a third-place play-off.

Against Switzerland, Gareth made some changes to his line-up, but not to his formation. England were sticking with the 4–3–3, even if hadn't led them to Nations League glory. They hit the post twice and had another goal harshly disallowed, but after 120 minutes it was still 0–0. The game was going to… PENALTIES!

Marcus was injured and Harry Kane had been subbed off, but Gareth had full faith in England's new spot-kick heroes:

Harry Maguire… scored!

Ross… scored!

Jadon… scored!

Raheem… scored!

Jordan Pickford… scored!

Eric… scored!

Six out of six, and Jordan then made a super save to win the shoot-out for England.

Hurraaaaaaaaay!

Although the result didn't really matter, Gareth still celebrated with his coaches on the sidelines. Because every England victory was a confidence boost and a stepping stone on the road to Euro 2020.

CHAPTER 22

EURO 2020: ANOTHER EXCITING STEP FORWARD

Due to the COVID-19 pandemic, Euro 2020 actually ended up taking place in 2021 instead. A year was a long time in football and the delay made a big difference to Gareth's final squad for the tournament. There were still plenty of familiar faces from the 2018 World Cup in Russia –

The two Harrys, Kane and Maguire, the two Jordans, Pickford and Henderson, Kyle, John, Kieran, Raheem, Marcus...

...But also lots of fresh new ones too:

Goalkeepers Aaron Ramsdale and Sam Johnstone;

Defenders Luke Shaw, Ben Chilwell, Conor Coady, Reece James, Ben White and Tyrone Mings;

Midfielders Declan Rice, Kalvin Phillips, Mason Mount and Jude Bellingham;

And attackers Jack Grealish, Jadon Sancho, Phil Foden, Dominic Calvert-Lewin and Bukayo Saka.

What an exciting young England squad it was, packed with so much pace and skill. Were they ready to go one step further than the heroes of 2018 and reach the Euro 2020 final? It would be played at Wembley, after all!

'I've got to try to manage the expectations for the players,' Gareth calmly told the media as the buzz began to build across the country. 'I accept the situation as a manager, there's expectation, I have to deliver.'

Before they could start thinking about semi-finals and finals, England needed to get their preparation right. Just like in 2018, Gareth wanted to create a good balance between hard work and fun, between training and team bonding. So, after their long practice sessions, the players were able to relax and recover together in a yoga pod, the swimming pool, or even on the basketball court.

'Mate, I'm glad you're shooting is better on the

football pitch!' Declan joked with Mason, his best
friend since they were kids.

Team spirit? *Tick!*

A strong mindset? *Tick!* England had qualified
for the Euros with seven wins out of eight, and in
their two friendlies before the tournament, they beat
Austria and Romania 1–0. Two cleansheets and two
more victories – the perfect preparation!

Right, England were ready to go. First up: another
rematch against Croatia.

Ahead of the game, Gareth had some difficult
decisions to make because there were so many
talented players competing for every position.

With Harry Maguire still injured, who should start
alongside John – Conor, Tyrone, or Ben White? Gareth
picked Tyrone for his height and power.

And what about the left-back spot – Luke or Ben
Chilwell? In the end, Gareth went for Kieran instead
because he was a better defender and he added more
experience to the team.

In midfield, Gareth selected Declan and Kalvin
in the deeper roles and Mason Mount as the more

attacking option.

And finally, who would England's third forward be – Harry Kane, Raheem and who? At the World Cup three years earlier, Gareth had stuck to the same team and same formation for every game, but now at the Euros, he was determined to be more adaptable. After hours of discussion, he decided that Phil was the best player for this particular match.

It nearly turned out to be a stroke of total genius. In the sixth minute, Phil cut inside and curled a fantastic shot towards the bottom corner... but no, it hit the post. So close to a dream start!

In the end, England had to wait until the second half to score. Kalvin burst forward and slid a great pass through to Raheem, who fired the ball past the Croatia keeper. *1–0!*

Hurraaaaaaaaay!

Wembley was less than a quarter full due to COVID-19 rules, but the fans made lots of noise as the goal went in, and so did Gareth. 'Yesssssssssss!' he yelled, pumping his fists with passion.

Now, England needed to defend well and hold

on for the win. Gareth had learned a lot from his World Cup experience, and so with ten minutes to go, he made a bold manager's decision: he took off his captain, Harry, and brought on Jude to add more energy in the midfield battle.

Together, the England players stayed strong until the very end, and with a final score of 1–0, they were off to a winning start! First challenge completed, now onto the next: beating their local rivals.

Other than switching to more attacking full-backs Reece and Luke, Gareth kept the same team against Scotland. England, however, didn't create enough chances, and the derby match ended in a 0–0 draw, much to the disappointment of the fans.

Where's the creativity? They're so boring to watch!

Get rid of Kane – he's rubbish!

Come on, Southgate – Grealish should be starting!

Gareth was now under real pressure to make changes for England's final group game against the Czech Republic. He didn't drop his captain, but he did bring in Jack and Bukayo for Mason and Phil. Could they add more energy and excitement to the attack?

Yes! Raheem hit the post in the second minute, and in the eleventh minute, he gave England the lead. The move started with Bukayo speeding up the right wing and it ended with Jack crossing it in from the left for Raheem to head home. *1–0!*

Hurraaaaaaaaay!

'That's more like it!' Gareth smiled to himself as he clapped on the sidelines. His changes had made an immediate impact.

Despite creating lots more chances, England failed to add to their one goal. Still, with two wins and a draw, and zero goals conceded, they topped their group to set up a Round of 16 tie against... Germany!

Noooooo, not again! That's what most England fans were thinking, but Gareth was feeling excited about the game. It would be a good test for his team and he really believed they could win it, as long as they got their tactics right.

So, what would be the best line-up for this particular match? They were already looking really hard to beat, but to make his defence even stronger, Gareth decided to switch from 4–3–3 to 3–4–3. That way, their formation would match Germany's.

For the first seventy minutes, it was a very tense and even battle, but then Gareth made a substitution that changed the whole game: Bukayo off, and Jack on. Suddenly, England's forwards seemed to come alive and the attacking football flowed.

Raheem passed forward to Harry Kane, who passed back to Jack, who passed left to Luke, who crossed it into the middle for Raheem. *1–0!*

Hurraaaaaaaaay!

Then ten minutes later, Luke passed left to Jack, who curled in another lovely left-foot cross for Harry to head home. *2–0!*

HURRAAAAAAAAAY!

The 40,000 England fans at Wembley went wild and so did the players on the pitch. They were on their way to the Euro 2020 quarter-finals!

'It's coming home, it's coming home,
It's coming, FOOTBALL'S COMING HOME!'

Gareth, however, wasn't getting carried away.

Beating Germany was a brilliant achievement, but England still had a long way to go. They had to take things one game at a time, starting with the quarter-final against Ukraine...

Raheem slipped a perfect pass through to Harry Kane, who had found his shooting boots again at last. *1–0!*

Luke curled the ball into the box and Harry Maguire headed it hard into the bottom corner. *2–0!*

Raheem flicked a pass to Luke, who crossed to Harry Kane. *3–0!*

From Mason's corner, Jordan Henderson scored his first-ever England goal. *4–0!*

Wow, Gareth's brave Young Lions were looking unstoppable! But no, it was still too soon for England to get over-excited. To reach their first-ever Euro final, they first had to get past Denmark, one of the strongest teams in the tournament.

After a tight opening thirty minutes, it was Denmark who took the lead, through a free kick from Mikkel Damsgaard. *1–0!*

Right, it was the first real test of England's togetherness and mindset at Euro 2020. How would Gareth's team bounce back after conceding their first goal in the whole tournament? 'Brilliantly!' was the answer. Just nine minutes after going behind, Bukayo fired a cross into the six-yard box, where he knew Raheem would be waiting. The final touch came off a sliding defender, but who cared? England were level – *1–1!*

'Come onnnnnnn!' Gareth cried out as he punched the air. He was really proud of his players for fighting back so quickly. Now, what about a winning goal?

Gareth brought on Jack after seventy minutes, like he had against Germany, but he couldn't find a way to become England's super sub again, and neither could Phil, who came on in extra-time. But just when the semi-final looked like it might be heading for a shoot-out, Raheem dribbled his way into the box, past one Denmark defender, and as he glided past another, he was barged in the side. *Penalty!*

Harry's spot-kick was saved, but fortunately he reacted quickly to score the rebound. *2–1!*

HURRAAAAAAAAAY!

There were still fifteen minutes to go, but the England defence didn't drop deeper and deeper like they had in the past. They had learned from that mistake. Instead, they kept the ball and calmly passed it around until at last the final whistle blew. They had done it; for the first time since 1966, England were through to the final of a major tournament!

After lots of emotional hugs and high-fives, Gareth and the players joined the fans for a special Wembley singalong:

'It's coming home, it's coming home,
It's coming, FOOTBALL'S COMING HOME!'

'Sweet Caroline,
Da-da-da,
Good times never seemed so good,
So good, so good, so good!'

What a night, and hopefully, there would be an even better night to come once England won the Euro 2020 final!

Beating Italy, however, was going to be their toughest challenge yet. The *Azzurri* had been brilliant all tournament, knocking out Belgium and Spain on their way to the final. But with the Wembley crowd cheering them on, England believed they could beat anyone, as long as they got their tactics right.

Gareth decided to go with a 3–4–3 again to make his team more solid, and his wing-backs made an instant impact. In the second minute of the match, Kieran sprinted up the right wing and crossed the ball to Luke, who volleyed it in at the back post. *1–0!*

Hurraaaaaaaaay!

Wow, another amazing start! Gareth, however, didn't even smile. One quick fist pump was his only celebration, and then he went back to coaching his players.

'Right, now keep your concentration!'

Unfortunately, it turned out to be the Croatia World Cup semi-final all over again. As the game went on, Italy grew stronger and stronger and England dropped deeper and deeper, until eventually the equaliser arrived. Bryan Cristante flicked on a corner at the front post and the ball bounced all the way through to Marco Verratti at the back. His header hit the post, but Leonardo Bonucci was there to smash the rebound past Harry Kane on the goal-line. *1–1!*

Nooooooooooooooo! What now – should England go for the winning goal, or stay solid at the back? In the end, Gareth decided to try a bit of both. He brought on Bukayo for Kieran to add speed to the attack, and also Jordan Henderson for Declan to add fresh legs in midfield.

England bounced back well and stayed strong for the final twenty minutes, and through the thirty minutes of extra-time too. The Euro 2020 final was going to… PENALTIES!

There was no need to panic, though. The England players had prepared long and hard for this moment, and Gareth felt confident about who his five best takers were:

1) Harry Kane… scored!

Yesssssssssssss!

2) Harry Maguire… scored!

Yesssssssssssss!

3) Marcus… hit the post!

Nooooooooooo!

4) Jadon… had his shot saved!

Noooooooooo!

5) Bukayo… had his shot saved too!

NOOOOOOOOO!

It was all over and Italy, not England, were the Euro 2020 winners. As the Azzurri celebrated, Gareth rushed over to comfort his heartbroken players and take responsibility, as always.

'Remember, we win together and lose together,' he told Marcus, Jadon and Bukayo. 'It was my decision for you to take those penalties and you were brave enough to step forward when I asked you to. So, be proud of yourselves and don't worry, we'll be back!'

No, England weren't the new European Champions, but with their winning smiles, strong principles, and superb performances on the pitch, they had united the nation again. And although it was hard for them to see the positives in that painful moment, they had also taken another exciting step forward, from semi-finalists at the 2018 World Cup to finalists at Euro 2020. What next – World Cup winners in 2022? Yes, that was the next step in Gareth's grand England plan.

Read on for a sneak preview of
another brilliant football story by
Matt and Tom Oldfield. . .

KANE

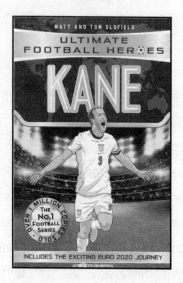

Available now!

CHAPTER 1

ENGLAND
HERO

Thursday, 5 October 2017

In the Wembley tunnel, Harry closed his eyes and soaked up the amazing atmosphere. He was back at the home of football, the stadium where he had first achieved his childhood dream of playing for England. 19 March 2015, England vs Lithuania – he remembered that game like it was yesterday. He had scored that day and now, with England facing Slovenia, he needed to do it again. As England's captain and Number 9, it was his job to shoot them to the 2018 World Cup.

'Come on, lads!' Harry called out to his teammates

behind him: friends like Joe Hart, Kyle Walker and Eric Dier. It was a real honour to be their leader. With a victory over Slovenia, they would all be on their way to the biggest tournament of their lives in Russia.

Harry looked down at the young mascot by his side and smiled at him. 'Right, let's do this!'

As the two of them led the England team out onto the pitch, the fans clapped and cheered. Harry didn't look up at the thousands of faces and flags; instead, he looked down at the grass in front of him. He was totally focused on his task: scoring goals and beating Slovenia.

'If you get a chance, test the keeper,' Harry said to his partners in attack, Raheem Sterling and Marcus Rashford, before kick-off. 'I'll be there for the rebound!'

Harry's new Premiership season with Tottenham Hotspur had not begun well in August, but by September he was back to his lethal best. That month alone, he scored an incredible thirteen goals, including two goals for England against Malta. He could score every type of goal – tap-ins, headers, one-on-ones, long-range shots, penalties, even free kicks. That's what made him such a dangerous striker.

With Slovenia defending well, Harry didn't get many chances in the first half. He got in good positions but the final ball never arrived.

'There's no need to panic yet,' Harry told his teammates in the dressing room. He really didn't want a repeat of England's terrible performance against Iceland at Euro 2016. That match still haunted him. 'We're good enough to win this by playing our natural game. Be patient!'

As Ryan Bertrand dribbled down the left wing, Harry sprinted towards the six-yard box. Ryan's cross didn't reach him but the ball fell to Raheem instead. His shot was going in until a defender deflected it wide.

'Unlucky!' Harry shouted, putting his hands on his head. 'Keep going, we're going to score!'

Without this kind of strong self-belief, Harry would never have made it to the top of European football. There had been lots of setbacks along the way: rejections, disappointments and bad form. But every time, Harry bounced back with crucial goals at crucial moments. That's what made him such a superstar.

A matter of seconds later, a rebound fell to him on the edge of the penalty area. Surely, this was his moment. He pulled back his left foot and curled a powerful shot towards the bottom corner. The fans were already up on their feet, ready to celebrate. Harry never missed... but this time he did. The ball flew just wide of the post. Harry couldn't believe it. He looked up at the sky and sighed.

On the sidelines, England manager Gareth Southgate cheered his team on. 'That's much better – the goal is coming, lads!'

But after ninety minutes, the goal still hadn't come. The fourth official raised his board: eight minutes of injury time.

'It's not over yet, boys!' Harry shouted, to inspire his teammates.

The Slovenian goalkeeper tried to throw the ball out to his left-back but Kyle got there first. Straight away, Harry was on the move from the back post to the front post. After playing together for years at Tottenham, they knew how to score great goals.

As Kyle crossed it in, Harry used his burst of speed to get in front of the centre-back. Again, the England supporters stood and waited anxiously. The ball was perfect and Harry stretched out his long right leg to meet it. The keeper got a touch on his shot but he couldn't keep it out.

Gooooooooooooaaaaaaaaaaaaaaaaaaaalllllllllllllllllllllllll llllll!!!!!!!!!!!!!!!!!!!!!!!

He had done it! Joy, relief, pride – Harry felt every emotion as he ran towards the fans. This time, he hadn't let them down. He held up the Three Lions on his shirt and screamed until his throat got sore.

'Captain to the rescue!' Kyle laughed as they hugged by the corner flag.

'No, it was all thanks to you!' Harry replied.

At the final whistle, he threw his arms up in the air. It was a phenomenal feeling to qualify for the 2018 World Cup. He couldn't wait to lead England to glory.

'We are off to Russia!' a voice shouted over the loudspeakers and the whole stadium cheered.

It was yet another moment that Harry would

never forget. Against the odds, he was making his childhood dreams come true. He was the star striker for Tottenham, the club that he had supported all his life. And now, like his hero David Beckham, he was the captain of England.

Harry had never given up, even when it looked like he wouldn't make it as a professional footballer. With the support of his family and his coaches, and lots of hard work and dedication, he had proved everyone wrong to become a world-class goal machine.

It had been an incredible journey from Walthamstow to Wembley, and Harry was only just getting started.

GARETH SOUTHGATE HONOURS

PLAYER

Crystal Palace

🏆 Football League
First Division:
1993–94

Aston Villa

🏆 League Cup:
1995–96

Middlesbrough

🏆 League Cup:
2003–04

MANAGER

England U-21

🏆 Toulon Tournament:
2016

Individual

🏆 Premier League
Manager of the Month:
August 2008

🏆 BBC Sports Personality
of the Year Coach
Award: 2018 and 2021

SOUTHGATE

THE FACTS

NAME: Gareth Southgate

DATE OF BIRTH: 3rd September 1970

PLACE OF BIRTH: Watford

NATIONALITY: English

PLAYING POSTION: CB

CURRENT JOB: England Manager

THE STATS

Height (cm):	183
Club appearances:	638
Club goals:	35
International appearances:	57
International goals:	2
Trophies as a player:	3
Trophies as a manager:	1

★ ★ ★ **HERO RATING: 87** ★ ★ ★

GREATEST MOMENTS

24 MARCH 1996,
ASTON VILLA 3–0 LEEDS UNITED

This was a very proud day for Gareth as part of Villa's brilliant back three. Together with Ugo Ehiogu and Paul McGrath, he marked Leeds' star striker Tony Yeboah out of the League Cup Final at Wembley. Then at the other end, Villa's forwards scored the goals to lead the team to cup glory. Gareth had moved to Villa to win trophies, and now he had achieved his aim!

15 JUNE 1998, ENGLAND 2–0 TUNISIA

Gareth had already achieved his dream of playing for England, but this match was extra special because it was his first time representing his country in a World Cup. What a feeling! A comfortable victory and a cleansheet was the perfect way to celebrate, especially after Gareth had bounced back from his penalty miss at Euro 96.

29 FEBRUARY 2004, BOLTON WANDERERS 1–2 MIDDLESBROUGH

This was a huge moment for Gareth and for his football club too. After taking an early 2–0 lead in the final, Middlesbrough held on to win the League Cup, their first major trophy in 128 years. And as captain, Gareth had the honour of lifting it high into the sky!

3 JULY 2018, ENGLAND 1–1 COLOMBIA (WON 4–3 ON PENALTIES)

In this World Cup Round of 16 clash, England were seconds away from winning 1–0, until Colombia equalised late in injury time. But Gareth's players picked themselves back up and, thanks to lots of practice and preparation, they won the shoot-out, ending England's twenty-eight years of penalty pain.

7 JULY 2021, ENGLAND 2–1 DENMARK

After losing in the World Cup semi-finals in 2018, Gareth's England took another exciting step forward three years later by beating Denmark and reaching the Euro 2020 final. His brave Young Lions fought back from 1–0 down in the semi-final, with Harry Kane scoring the winning goal in extra-time. Hurray – Gareth had guided England to their first major tournament final since 1966!

PLAY LIKE YOUR HEROES

GUIDE YOUR TEAM TO SUCCESS
LIKE GARETH SOUTHGATE

STEP 1: Be kind. No-one likes a scary manager! Make sure you take the time to talk to your players and get to know them properly as people.

STEP 2: Stay calm. No-one likes a shouty manager either! If something goes wrong, there's no point getting angry. Instead, spend your time thinking about ways to improve the situation.

STEP 3: Dress smart. A waistcoat and suit might not be your style, but no-one wants a manager who looks like they've just got out of bed!

STEP 4: Prepare well. You need to make sure that your players feel ready and raring to go, both physically and mentally. That takes lots of practice and encouragement.

STEP 5: Teamwork makes the dream work, and it's okay to have a bit of fun! Find ways to build a bond between your players, whether that's a tough trip away with the Royal Marines, inflatable unicorns in a swimming pool, or something totally different.

STEP 6: Celebrate success. GOAL! If your team scores early in the game, keep your 'Yesssssss!' quick and quiet, but if there's not much time left, throw both arms up and punch the air with passion.

TEST YOUR KNOWLEDGE

QUESTIONS

1. What sports did Gareth's parents play when they were younger?

2. Which Manchester United and England player was Gareth's childhood hero?

3. Which future England teammate did Gareth train with at the Southampton academy?

4. True or false – Gareth scored on his Premier League debut?

5. How many times did Gareth get relegated with Crystal Palace?

6. Who were the other two members of Villa's brilliant back three?

7. Which England player put his arm around Gareth when he missed 'that' penalty at Euro 96?

8. How many times did Gareth win the League Cup as a player?

9. How many clubs did Gareth captain as a player?

10. Which formation did Gareth's England team play at the 2018 World Cup?

11. At Euro 2020, who did Gareth bring on against Germany to change the game?

1. *They were both athletes – his dad threw the javelin and his mum ran the hurdles.* 2. *Bryan Robson.* 3. *Alan Shearer.* 4. *True, and it was a worldie, for Crystal Palace vs Blackburn!* 5. *Two (but he also got them promoted in between!).* 6. *Ugo Ehiogu and Paul McGrath.* 7. *Stuart Pearce.* 8. *Two.* 9. *All three – Crystal Palace, Aston Villa and Middlesbrough.* 10. *3–5–2.* 11. *Jack Grealish.*